Rose
and the
Lost Princess

HOLLY WEBB

sourcebooks
jabberwocky

Copyright © 2010 by Holly Webb
Cover and internal design © 2014 by Sourcebooks, Inc.
Cover design by Jane Archer
Cover illustration © Kevin Keele

Sourcebooks and the colophon are registered trademarks of Sourcebooks, Inc.

Published by Sourcebooks Jabberwocky, an imprint of Sourcebooks, Inc.
P.O. Box 4410, Naperville, Illinois 60567-4410
(630) 961-3900
Fax: (630) 961-2168
www.jabberwockykids.com

Originally published in 2010 in the United Kingdom by Orchard Books, a division of Hachette Children's Books.

Library of Congress Cataloging-in-Publication data is on file with the publisher.

Source of Production: Versa Press, East Peoria, Illinois
Date of Production: February 2014
Run Number: 5000582

Printed and bound in the United States of America.
VP 10 9 8 7 6 5 4 3 2 1

For Jon

One

ENJOYING THE QUIET, ROSE leaned against the window, staring out at the last few browning leaves of the wisteria that climbed up the wall and feeling the smooth chill of the glass against her cheek.

She jumped as a soft, insistent white head butted against her arm, and Gus squirmed into her lap, kneading her apron to the right consistency with determined paws.

"It's getting colder," he remarked, settling down at last. "I can smell snow."

Rose blinked at him, surprised. "Do you think so? It's only October. Isn't it a bit early for snow?"

Gus wriggled onto his back and yawned, showing a bright pink tongue and shark-like teeth. His stomach was round and soft and tufty, framed by delicately hanging paws. Rose was tempted to stroke it but suspected that Gus might claw her for being overly familiar.

"You can if you like," he purred, opening his orange eye for a moment. "I'm in a tolerant mood."

Rose stroked one of the velvet paws with the back of her hand instead and sighed.

"What's the matter?" Gus asked, opening the blue eye this time, just for a second.

"Just tired…" Rose murmured.

Gus sniffed irritably and opened both eyes to glare at her. "Well, it's entirely your own fault for being so ridiculously stubborn. Why you persist in working as a housemaid and trying to be a magician's apprentice at the same time is completely beyond me. You have to choose one or the other."

Rose didn't answer. He'd said it several times, and today she felt weary enough to wonder if he was actually right. He quite often was, having a cat's natural cunning coupled with a hefty dollop of magic. But it still seemed odd, being advised by a cat.

"You see! I was right," Gus mewed triumphantly, now standing on her lap with his front paws resting against the glass.

Rose, who had been staring out the window but not actually looking, shook herself and gazed out at the trees in the square's garden. The color had bled out of the sky, and fat white snowflakes were swirling slowly down.

"It's snowing!" Freddie burst into the room, flinging the door open with a bang. "Do you see? Really snowing. And it's cold enough to stick."

Rose looked at him in surprise. His dark eyes were

glittering with excitement, and his cheeks were flushed, as though he'd raced up the stairs. It was only snow, and Rose didn't think she liked it all that much. It was beautiful but somehow menacing too—the falling flakes had a horrid inevitability about them, as though they would keep falling whatever happened and smother anything that tried to stop them. Rose shook herself crossly. This was nonsense. It was snow. Just weather.

"Aren't you pleased?" Freddie asked her, frowning slightly. "It's snowing!" The frown disappeared as he said the word, as if he couldn't mention snow without grinning.

Rose watched him dubiously as he pressed his palms against the window, gazing hungrily out at the dancing feathers of snow. Why was he so excited? It snowed every year, as far as she knew. For an orphanage brat, snow didn't mean treats. It just meant that your dormitory was so cold you climbed into bed with the girls next to you, so you could shiver together. And the washing water froze. When the orphans walked to church in snow, no one threw snowballs; they just got wet feet, as the dirty slush seeped through their patched boots. She supposed this was the difference. For Freddie, snow probably meant snow fights and sledding and riding out to the country to skate on a beautiful frozen lake. He probably came home and had cocoa afterward too.

"It looks very cold," Rose told him rather primly, and he shook his head.

"Honestly, Rose, you really are the most dreadful wet blanket," Freddie murmured dismissively as he watched the snowflakes, unable to tear himself away.

Rose smiled. Sometimes it annoyed her that Freddie had no idea how lucky he was, how privileged. But it wasn't actually his fault. He just happened to have been born that way—to a family with a long history of magic. And money. Just as she happened to have been born to a family so poor they couldn't keep her. Or maybe not a family—she didn't know. Perhaps just a girl on her own, a girl who'd found an old fish basket somewhere and used it to shelter the baby she was abandoning in the churchyard.

When she wasn't exhausted, Rose felt privileged too. She had been taken away from the orphanage at a far younger age than most the girls, to be trained as a housemaid in the London residence of Mr. Aloysius Fountain, Chief Magical Counselor to the Treasury. Rose loved it. She had dreamed of this—a proper job, no more charity, but actually earning her own living. Then she had discovered that she was a little bit magical too, and everything had changed all over again.

It seemed odd that two people with such different childhoods should end up as apprentices together. Rose wasn't on the same social scale as Freddie, of course. Most probably she never would be. But she was better at a lot of the magic than he was. That was hard to believe too. It almost certainly meant that at least one of her unknown parents had been a magician. Since Mr. Fountain had gently pointed this out in their first magic lesson, Rose had thought about her parents far more than she ever had before. She knew something about them now—or one of them, at least. Before, all she'd known was a possible connection with fish. Having inherited her magic was far more interesting than having inherited fish.

She had never daydreamed about her parents back at the orphanage, as so many of her friends did. No, far better to rely on herself, as she always had. She shouldn't waste time wondering; she would never know the answers anyway. Unless she could divine them somehow, of course. One of her new powers was making strange pictures appear on shiny surfaces. Some of the images were true, and some were…Rose wasn't quite sure what. Perhaps they all had some sort of truth in them, or they wouldn't come to her.

Could she see her parents? If she tried hard enough, found the right place to look? Did she even want to? Rose wasn't sure she wanted to know why they'd left her on the war memorial. What if they just hadn't liked her very much? Or something awful had happened to them?

But the more Rose found out about her own magic, the more intriguing her family history was becoming.

Left alone in Mr. Fountain's workroom, she'd found herself staring at mirrors, silver bowls, that strange mother-of-pearl sheet…She knew she could see in all of them if she could only bring herself to try.

"I wish he'd hurry up. I want to go out before it gets dark. Where is he, Rose? Do you know? Rose!" Freddie's voice grew sharp, and Rose turned away from the mesmerizing snowflakes with a guilty start.

"What?"

"Where is Mr. Fountain?" Freddie demanded impatiently. "It's twenty minutes past three. What's he doing? Come on, Rose, down in the kitchens you know everything! Where is he?"

"He had a lunch guest, someone from the palace. Miss Bridges was panicking, and me and Bill had to polish all the silver yesterday. She checked. Even the bits we never use, like that strange cup with the mustache on it." Rose sounded disgruntled. Bill, the apprentice footman who did all the odd jobs around the house, had confided to her on her first day that although they were supposed to polish all the silver every week, he never did, except on very special occasions. Visitors from the palace, even if not actually royalty themselves, clearly had to be treated like royalty, and that meant everything needed to be shiny.

Freddie looked thoughtful. "I wonder who it is. My cousin Raphael is an equerry at the palace, so I know some of the staff."

Rose gazed at him wide-eyed. "Your cousin works for the king? What's an equerry?"

Freddie sniffed. "An odd-job man, judging by Raphael. But he's a bit of an idiot. In a dream world all the time, and he isn't even a magician. He's from my mother's side of the family."

Rose couldn't help giggling. Someone that Freddie thought was stupid would have to be monumentally silly. Freddie fell down flights of stairs on purpose to see if he could fly. (He had, almost, but it was still a stupid thing to do. He said it was in the spirit of scientific inquiry and scientists had to be willing to take risks. Rose just thought he was bacon brained.) But Freddie had raised an interesting point.

"So, your mother's not a magician, then?" she asked curiously. "Only your father?"

"Yes." Freddie smiled. "But Mama loves magic. My father courted her by making roses grow out of the carpet of my grandparents' drawing room, and she accepted his proposal on the spot. Not that she might have turned him down," he hastened to add. "Papa has very handsome side whiskers."

Rose couldn't stop laughing. She imagined Freddie's father rather like Freddie, smooth and small and blond, but with luxuriant muttonchop whiskers.

"Stop it, Rose! I can hear Fountain coming." Freddie frowned at her, still giggling in the window seat, and shook his head disgustedly.

Rose sat up and tried to take deep breaths, but the image of a furry Freddie wouldn't go away. At last, the turning of the door handle distracted her enough, and she jumped up excitedly. She adored their magic lessons, however tired she was, and Mr. Fountain had promised to teach Freddie and Rose a real spell today. Rose dug her fingernails into her palms. She wanted to be as calm and collected as Freddie, who'd rather be out throwing snowballs than learning magic, but she could hardly stand still. She could smell Mr. Fountain, she suddenly realized, as the door opened. A mixture of cigar smoke, very dear eau de cologne, and an added tang of powerful, lethal, wonderful magic…

Two

I T HAD ONLY BEEN a week since Rose and Freddie and Mr. Fountain's spoiled little princess of a daughter, Isabella, had set out on a mission to rescue one of Rose's friends who had gone missing from the orphanage. Freddie and Rose hadn't wanted to take Isabella, but she could be very persuasive, combining all the usual talents of a spoiled child with a rather large magical inheritance. It was extremely hard to say no to her, and most people just didn't bother.

Maisie had been kidnapped by another magician, an evil madwoman trying to discover the secret of eternal life by drinking children's blood. As Mr. Fountain had explained to them afterward (along with dire threats never to go off and do anything so infernally stupid ever again, at least not without telling him first), it was a quest that tended to warp people's minds. Magicians seeking the power of life and death went absolutely batty, it seemed, "mad as a spoon," as Mr. Fountain put it.

Miss Sparrow had been much madder than that. She had been maddened enough to murder, and she slit children's wrists to harvest their blood for her infernal plans. She didn't even kill them cleanly—she kept them alive, like little milk cows in her cellar, so she could do it again and again and again. She'd had Maisie's blood, and that of fifteen other stolen children. She'd been working on Rose and Freddie and Bella, but thankfully they'd escaped before she had set on them with her sparkly silver knife.

Rose had used magic to save Maisie and all the others, but she'd lost her secret. After she and Freddie came back to the house in triumph, on the heels of a ragged gang of lost children, she hadn't been able to hide it any longer. Not when Freddie and Gus had spilled her story to Mr. Fountain, and he insisted on her becoming another apprentice. It was wonderful upstairs in the drawing room, for all of two hours. Mr. Fountain promised that she could still be a maid as well. Rose hadn't wanted to change worlds completely. She'd spent her life at the orphanage dreaming of a job where she could work for money, where she wasn't a little charity girl. She wasn't going to give it up yet.

None of the servants had gone to bed—they couldn't anyway, with the drawing room full of stolen children and the police upstairs demanding tea at all hours. Miss Bridges, the housekeeper, was in her little room, writing a list of houses that she thought might take the orphans and street children into service, and Mrs. Jones and Sarah, the kitchen maid, were making towering piles of sandwiches. Miss Sparrow had fed the children in her cellar, but only to the extent of throwing in a couple of loaves every day. The first batch of sandwiches Mrs. Jones sent up had disappeared in seconds, and now she was thinking that they might need to bake some more bread.

Bill wasn't there—he and the stableboy had been sent off with messages to the parents of the children who'd been stolen from their homes. He had known already anyway; he'd seen Rose in action, when she'd done magic by accident, and at first he'd been angry with her. He'd forgiven her now, especially since one of the children she'd rescued had been a friend of his from St. Bartholomew's, the orphanage on the other side of the wall from where Rose had lived. Rose had saved Jack, so Bill was willing to give her the benefit of the doubt.

Susan, the upper housemaid, who spent most of her time making life unpleasant for Rose—far more time than she spent working—looked up at her as she came into the kitchen. "Oh, so you've decided to come back down and do some work now, have you, instead of getting in the way upstairs? Bill says you went out and got into some fight with a magician!" Susan sneered. "You'll be dismissed for sure." She'd been pressed into making sandwiches as well, and she brandished a butter knife at Rose, her eyes glittering with excitement. She loved getting other people into trouble.

Rose stared at her. Susan's sharply pretty face was distorted by resentment and jealousy. She noticed for the first time that little sour lines were setting in around her mouth and nose. "Mr. Fountain asked me to stay," she murmured, looking away.

"Rose, what were you doing out there?" Mrs. Jones demanded, looking fretfully at her over a pile of her precious jars of jam. "You weren't here for dinner; we were worried. I thought you might have gone back to the orphanage, seeing as some people weren't as well-behaved to you as they should have been." She put the jars down on the kitchen table and glared at Susan, who calmly licked butter off her fingers. "And then you came back with Mr. Freddie and Miss Isabella! What were you thinking of, Rose? You should never let those strange children bully you into doing who knows what!"

"It wasn't like that…" Rose started to say, but she didn't know how to explain. Besides, she felt a tiny spark of anger growing inside her, which made it hard to be polite. Freddie and Bella weren't strange! Well, yes, maybe they were—in fact, of course they were. But no more than Rose herself was! What was "normal," anyway, if a little half-starved pauper girl from an orphanage could turn out to be a magician?

"You're a servant, Rose dear." Mrs. Jones's face was

anxious, and Rose's momentary anger faded. She didn't want Mrs. Jones to look like that because of her. The cook had been kind to her ever since she had arrived.

"Don't go getting mixed up with those children. Never forget, they could have you dismissed with one word! One complaint, Rose, and then where would you be? Be careful, dear." Mrs. Jones stared at her, her cheeks red with sincerity.

Miss Bridges appeared in the doorway from the passage that led to her room, the yard, and the stables in the mews. Susan suddenly started buttering bread again, rather quickly, and Rose looked around for something to hold so she could at least try and look busy.

Miss Bridges wasn't scared of magic. She had far more to do with Mr. Fountain than the rest of the servants, and she'd always thought there was something special about Rose anyway. Besides, Rose worked hard, and for Miss Bridges that was what mattered. The news she had been given earlier that evening, that Rose was to become an apprentice in her spare time, had merely made her smile grimly. She wondered what Mr. Fountain thought Rose did that she should have spare time. She had given her employer a regal nod and promised to organize Rose's duties to make room for her lessons with Freddie.

"Rose, what on earth are you doing with that cake stand? Put it down, girl. And come here."

It hadn't been the most sensible item to try to look

busy with, Rose realized, as she scurried across the kitchen, trying not to hear Susan sniggering. Miss Bridges put a hand on her shoulder and turned her to face the rest of the staff. "Rose has been—discovered," she said slowly.

Rose glanced up hastily and then down again as she saw an expression of unholy glee on Susan's face. She probably thought that Rose had been caught stealing or fraternizing with next-door's boot boy.

"As a result, she will now be having lessons in magic with Mr. Frederick in the afternoons," Miss Bridges continued smoothly. There was silence. Rose risked looking up again and saw that Sarah, Susan, and Mrs. Jones were all looking blank.

"You mean—she's one of them upstairs?" Mrs. Jones said at last, in a disbelieving voice. "Never! Not little Rose!" She sounded as though Rose had murdered someone. Perhaps the problem was that Rose *could*. Not that she wanted to, Rose added hurriedly to herself. She twisted her hands tightly together in front of her apron and tried not to look dangerous.

"But she's not born to it, Miss Bridges. This can't be right," Mrs. Jones said in a troubled voice. "Where did she get it from? She's spent too much time messing about with that Mr. Freddie!"

"I don't think that magic is catching, Mrs. Jones," Miss Bridges murmured soothingly. "I imagine that one of Rose's parents must have passed the trait on to her. We should be truly grateful that she has ended up in a house where her talent may be put to use. The workings of Providence, I'm sure you will agree."

Mrs. Jones didn't look as though she thought it was providential at all. She looked like she was about to explode, her face growing redder and redder with every minute.

"Who's going to do all her work?" Susan spat angrily. "Not me, that's for sure!" She caught Miss Bridges's steely eye and went back to buttering.

"Considering that you hardly manage to do your own work, I doubt very much that you will do any of Rose's," Miss Bridges said coldly. "Your opinion on the master's decision was not invited, strangely enough."

"Is this what you really want, Rose?" Mrs. Jones turned to her with hope in her eyes.

Rose nodded. She hated to disappoint Mrs. Jones, but she'd tried pretending that her magic didn't exist. It spilled over in unfortunate ways, and Rose thought it might get dangerous quite soon. Besides, she liked it. So far she hadn't done a great deal of magic, apart from the bits she'd had to do because mad lady magicians were trying to kill her and her friends. She hadn't had much time to enjoy those bits. But she had a feeling that magic lessons might be wonderful—she just hoped there wasn't too much bookwork before the real magic started. And that was without even thinking about the money—Freddie had told her just a little about what magicians could earn, and it had made Rose dizzy.

Mrs. Jones stared at her, shaking her head. Rose had a feeling that she didn't realize she was doing it. The red had drained out of her face, leaving it pale and grayish. Rose thought she knew partly why Mrs. Jones was so upset—although she still didn't understand why the cook disliked magic so. Mrs. Jones's baby, Maria Rose, had died of the cholera—and if she had lived, she would have been about the same age as Rose. For Mrs. Jones, having Rose had been like seeing her daughter grown up, even sharing a name. But now, another daughter was leaving her behind, and Mrs. Jones couldn't even bring herself to wish her well.

Why are they so afraid of it? Rose wondered to herself. No one had bothered much with magic at the orphanage—it was one of those expensive luxuries that no one really cared about. There were more important things missing, like food. All she could think was that it was living so close to magic that scared them: having it there just on the other side of the door to the servants' quarters and not knowing quite what it was—or what it wanted. That could turn your stomach, she supposed.

It didn't help that Gus liked to visit belowstairs for his daily treat of best Jersey cream, and he was so obviously not a normal cat. He delighted in looking supernatural and was a master at making knowing faces. Bill thought he was a devil.

The back door from the mews banged, and Bill sneaked in, damp with the fog. As soon as he saw Miss Bridges, he removed his hat and tried to look respectful. Unfortunately, taking his hat off made his scrubby mat of hair spring up, and any pretense of a well-trained, well-turned-out servant was gone. Miss Bridges flinched. She tried her best with Bill, and he actually did his job very well, but nothing was going to turn him into a polished footman. Ever. "Me and Jacob found them all, miss," he muttered. "They're coming."

"Good. At least a few of the poor waifs will go home tonight," Miss Bridges murmured. "Alert me when they arrive, Susan. And, Rose, you should go to bed. You will be very busy tomorrow, and you seem to have had an—unsettling experience."

Rose blinked at her until she realized that Miss Bridges meant being attacked by a mad enchantress. She supposed it *had* been rather unsettling.

Susan bobbed a curtsy, but her dark eyes were alive with malice, and she watched Miss Bridges eagerly as she left the room.

"I meant what I said," she hissed to Rose, as soon as the housekeeper had gone. "I won't be doing your share of the work while you're off gallivanting with that unnatural boy."

Bill gave a scornful laugh. "Work! When did you ever do any work?"

Susan turned on him, snakelike. "Well, you'll be

doing it then, won't you? All Rose's chores. While she's upstairs with Mr. *Freddie*." She smirked meanly, clearly expecting Bill to be jealous, but he only shrugged and smirked back.

"You watch your mouth, Susan. You haven't seen what she can do. I have. You don't wanna get on the wrong side of little Rose." He folded his arms triumphantly, but Mrs. Jones gasped.

"You've seen her do magic? You knew about this before tonight and you didn't say anything?"

Bill looked uncomfortable. "Nobody asked me nothing..." he muttered. "Didn't know I was supposed to."

"What did she do?" asked Sarah, the kitchen maid, with a sort of sick fascination.

Mrs. Jones tutted, but she didn't tell Bill to stop. She stared at him, being careful not to look at Rose.

Rose felt like telling them to ask *her*, but she decided now was probably not the time to draw any more attention to herself.

Bill grinned. "She poured treacle all over this bloke on a horse. He was yelling 'cause she nearly went in front of him, wandering along like a daft daisy. He tried to hit her."

"And she poured treacle on him?" Susan asked disbelievingly. "She didn't strike him with lightning or anything like that? Just treacle?"

"Was it good treacle?" Mrs. Jones gasped in distress.

18

"The quality kind? Or that nasty, grainy stuff we had once that I sent back?"

"Dunno." Bill shook his head. "It was sticky. Stuck to that white horse a treat."

"She isn't a proper witch," Susan said scornfully. "Just some little orphan half-breed. Who'd want her? A changeling, most likely."

Rose's heart swelled with pain. A changeling! A nasty little fairy child, made out of mud and spit? Maybe she was. After the excitement and terror of that night, she felt she could believe anything. And she knew she couldn't face any more.

Rose turned and ran out of the kitchen, biting her fingers to keep herself from letting Susan hear her cry.

"See?" She heard Susan laughing as she ran away. "She knows!"

Three

O VER THE DAYS THAT followed, Susan didn't become any less horrible about Rose and her magic. She lost no opportunity to make mean, spiteful little comments, which Rose knew she should just ignore but somehow couldn't quite. Susan had a knack for finding ideas that took root in Rose's mind. "Your parents abandoned you because you're a half-breed, I bet." And, "Maybe you were born a frog, did you think of that?"

But the magic made up for it. Rose could suffer Susan and her nastiness, as long as she had the magic. Rose had to hold on to it. That was why the lessons were so special—she was desperate to learn how it worked, why it worked. Rose was very keen on doing things properly, and everything magical that she had done so far had just happened. It almost felt as though it wasn't much to do with her at all.

"I'm sorry, my dears," Mr. Fountain sighed as he shut the workroom door distractedly. He was frowning, and his mustache was particularly pointy, which meant he had been twisting it, as he did when he was worried. Clearly the visit from the palace that morning had not been a welcome one.

"Who was it who came from the palace, sir?" Freddie asked curiously.

"Havers. The Lord Chamberlain," Mr. Fountain added as an aside to Rose. "Fussing about these idiotic protests. What does the stupid man think I'm going to do about it? Just because I'm their tame magician, they think I speak for all of us. Ridiculous."

"Protests?" Rose asked, frowning.

Mr. Fountain fingered his mustache and sighed.

"The news about Miss Sparrow has gotten out," he explained reluctantly. "Public reaction has been, shall we say, rather *extreme*…"

"I don't understand." Rose looked from Freddie to Gus to Mr. Fountain, her eyes wide with worry. "We saved them all. We didn't do anything wrong. I mean, we were going to break in, but we didn't even do that in the end, because she captured us." Then she swallowed. "Is it because we set that mist monster on her? We didn't know what else to do, honestly we didn't!"

Gus laughed—a low bitter sound—and stood up on her lap to bump her cheek lovingly. "They are not seeking to protect the witch, Rose."

Rose saw Mr. Fountain blink, and Freddie flinched, but Gus stared at them both sternly. "I only call her what she was."

21

"That's what everyone is calling her now, Gus." Mr. Fountain's face was equally stern. "And a great many worse names. And they're not just using them for her."

"All of us," Freddie whispered. "They think we're all like her—murderers, child killers, making up foul spells to steal people's souls." He shrugged. "Who knows what else."

"That's just the point." Mr. Fountain sighed. "They don't know. They just don't understand what we are, what we do. So they're thinking up the most fantastical, mad ideas, and rumors are running through the city like rainwater." He looked into Rose's frightened eyes and smiled a bright, rather unconvincing smile, rubbing his hands together briskly. "They'll forget… sooner or later…Magicians are too useful to lose. Don't worry, Rose. Work!"

He strode over to the table. Gus jumped off Rose's lap and bounded after him, springing up onto the table with a surprisingly athletic leap for such a portly cat. He sat in the middle of the table, his tail wrapped snugly around his paws, the tip just twitching with anticipation. His whiskers trembled eagerly. He adored magic and hated it when his master spent too much time at the palace. Mr. Fountain was the Chief Magical Counselor to the Treasury, which really just meant that he made them a lot of gold. But because he was at the palace so much, he had an unofficial role as the only magician the king actually knew. This was useful, in some ways, but rather time-consuming.

"What are we going to do?" Rose whispered, smoothing her hands down her apron, letting the scratchy feel of the starched cotton slow her jumpy heartbeat.

Freddie looked eagerly at the book Mr. Fountain was drawing down from the shelf. One of the odd, frightening, dark-leather ones, Rose noted uncertainly. Magic lessons so far—she had only had two—had been wonderful but not really magical. There had been no fireworks, no fizzing sparks. Nothing as exciting as the mist monster Freddie had conjured up to fight Miss Sparrow. Instead, they'd had interesting discussions on the powers of different metals and how lead boots had protective qualities. That sort of thing.

But she had a feeling that today was going to be different. With the snow falling outside and the promise of a real spell, the air in the workroom felt charged with excitement, and Gus's fur was spitting tiny little blue sparks.

Mr. Fountain laid the book on the table, opened it, and smoothed out the pages lovingly. Freddie and Rose leaned over curiously to read the title at the top of the page. It was handwritten in emerald-green ink. *The Theory and Practice of Weaving a Glamour Spell, With Some Personal Observations of My Own.*

"Who wrote it?" Rose asked, admiring the spiky, elegant handwriting.

"My own mentor, many years ago. He was particularly expert at glamours." Mr. Fountain smiled secretively, remembering.

Rose nodded, but she was frowning. "Freddie said glamours are terribly difficult," she murmured apologetically. "I don't know anything about them."

"There wouldn't be much point in me teaching you if you did," Mr. Fountain pointed out. "Glamours are actually relatively simple, but they are draining. Do you remember how you told me that Miss Sparrow lost her glamours when you attacked her? She could bring them back, but they were never quite as convincing after that, once you'd seen the real her underneath. Glamours have to be maintained; you can't let them slip. That's why they're so difficult to do."

"Strong magic," Freddie muttered, his dark eyes glowing. "How do we start?" He scanned the book eagerly, then looked up in surprise. "We just make up any incantation we like?"

Mr. Fountain nodded. "The words are more to help you concentrate than anything else. Repeating them keeps the glamour going."

Gus brushed his tail across the page, his luminous fur picking up a tinge of green light from that brilliant ink. "But you must know yourself before you can change," he whispered, "or who knows what you might come out as."

"What on earth does that mean?" Freddie asked sniffily. "I hate it when you go all mystical."

Gus eyed him with disfavor. "All mystical? Is that what you call it? You really are a most commonplace child."

"What Gus is trying to say," Mr. Fountain put in wearily, "is that you can't glamour yourself without a strong sense of who you really are. Your starting point. Here." He handed Freddie a small, silver-framed hand mirror. "Begin with something simple. Turn your eyes blue."

Freddie stared into the mirror, scowling, and Rose's heart thumped anxiously. After Freddie, she would have to try, and she had no idea who she really was. What if she couldn't do it? She loved the idea of glamours, becoming someone else, even for only a minute. Her whole life as an apprentice felt like some enormous magic trick as it was. But how much magic would be denied her because she hadn't a family to tell her who she had been? Freddie would gloat too, she thought.

"Have you thought of the words?" Mr. Fountain asked. "You can say them out loud if you like, though of course for a really convincing glamour, they have to be silent, or it's rather obvious what you're doing."

Freddie looked superior. "I'm already saying them. There! Don't my eyes look blue? A little?"

Rose peered at him. "No. Oh! Weren't you meant to change the brown part of your eyes?"

"What?" Freddie looked anxiously back to the mirror.

The whites of his eyes were slowly turning a rich, deep, glowing blue. It was a rather disturbing effect.

"You also have to be *accurate*..." Mr. Fountain pointed out. "But a good first try."

Freddie's eyes lost their strange color in a gentle fade, like rinsing the blue out of washing. He glared at Rose, as though daring her to do better than he had.

Rose blinked. She really had no idea what she was supposed to do. The book said just to see oneself with the required changes. But how? Freddie handed her the mirror and watched her, hawklike—a hawk with strangely bluish eyes.

Rose stared at her reflection. Her mirror-self looked pale and worried. Just seeing oneself differently didn't sound very clear. It sounded almost too easy, especially for someone who made moving pictures appear on anything shiny.

"Try changing the color of your hair," Mr. Fountain suggested to Rose, and she grimaced at her short, dark locks in the mirror. Orphans had their hair cut very short, to avoid lice, or at least to make lice easier to get rid of. Rose wasn't planning to cut hers again ever, but it would be a long time before she had luxuriant long hair like Isabella's. Rose smiled, imagining herself, seeing a new Rose in the mirror, with rose-petal soft cheeks and rich waves of golden hair rippling down her back. The kind of hair that needed a maid to brush it every night...

26

Long hair, long hair,
Long and fair…
Long hair, long hair,
Long and fair…
Long hair, long hair,
Long and fair…

Rose chanted it to herself silently, the rhythm bouncing through her brain.

"Rose, stop!" Gus's mew had an undertone of panic, and Rose reluctantly dragged her eyes away from the pretty filigree mirror. She gasped, a hand going to her mouth in shock and staying there to hide a smile.

Gus was blond. His fur was distinctly longer than usual, and it was a soft golden-toffee shade—much the same color as Freddie's hair, which was now waist length. Mr. Fountain's hair hadn't grown, but it was blond too, and so was his beautiful mustache, which was now hanging to his shoulders in two caramel-colored ringlets.

Rose glanced hopefully back into the mirror, anxious to see her own transformation. But her hair was the same dark brown as usual and not an inch longer.

"What did you do?" Freddie demanded indignantly. "Turn it back! Make it go away!"

Rose gave him a worried look. "Um. How?" she asked Mr. Fountain. "I don't actually know what I did, so I'm not sure how to undo it…"

Mr. Fountain was holding one end of his mustache and regarding it oddly, his expression half pained, half thoughtful. Surely he wasn't considering keeping it? At last he sighed and snapped his fingers regretfully. His mustache curled crisply back into its perfect pomaded points, Gus was snow white again, and Freddie had an extremely short haircut. Rose suspected the master had taken advantage of the opportunity to tidy him up a bit.

"I think we may need a little practice," Mr. Fountain said slowly.

Four

ROSE TRAILED DOWN THE stairs to the kitchen after the lesson, her head still half full of confusing power. Of course the glamour hadn't worked as it should, but she had done *something*! And the tingling, shimmering sensation of being surrounded by magic was still wonderful. She was too preoccupied to notice the sudden silence that fell as she walked into the kitchen. She sank into a chair and looked hopefully at the teapot that was standing on the big wooden kitchen table. She was tired, and just the sight of that snow falling outside the windows had made her feel cold. Freddie was right. It was sticking. She was dazed enough that when no cup of tea was passed across the table, she did not simply get up and go away, which was what she was meant to do.

Rose glanced up, a polite request on her lips, but then she met the expressions worn by the two other people at the table, and her thirst for tea died. She had almost forgotten. Everyone knew now, about the magic in her. They'd known for a week, but they didn't seem to have gotten used to the idea.

Rose had found the staff hard to understand when she first came to the Fountain house from the orphanage. For a start, she couldn't see how everyone in the lower part of the house managed to ignore its magical qualities so completely. For her, the stairs moved, the stuffed animals talked, and the furniture sparkled with magical history. Except in the kitchen, where Mrs. Jones refused to allow that nasty-tasting magic stuff.

Mrs. Jones had been one of Rose's favorite people in the house. She was kind, and she was a wonderful cook, and she gave Rose enormous portions to fatten her up. After a lifetime of orphanage food, where there was always just enough to get by but never so much that you felt full and a good two-thirds of most meals consisted of cabbage, Rose adored eating at the Fountain house. The dresses she'd made for herself when she arrived were already starting to feel somewhat snug around her middle. It was wonderful.

But Mrs. Jones had a very strange attitude toward magic. She tolerated it, as long as it stayed in its place, which was preferably well away from her. She didn't mind magical things, as long as they were big and expensive and difficult. But casual, easy magic—someone who could light the kitchen fire by looking at it—that was unnatural.

Rose had eventually come to realize that Mrs. Jones

only trusted magic if it was bought and sold. She'd even given Rose an amulet of protection a few weeks before. It was a complete sham, but she had meant well, and she had paid for it. Now that she knew Rose could protect herself, she was frightened, and that made her angry.

The events of the past week, her sudden pariah status among the servants, flashed back into Rose's weary mind with painful sharpness as she saw Sarah and Mrs. Jones watching her warily, as though she might smite them with something.

"All I wanted was a cup of tea," Rose said quietly, staring back.

Mrs. Jones looked upset, and Sarah clutched her cup as though the thick china handle was a lifeline. She was so scared that it broke, the handle parting company with the cup, and she shrieked and jumped up.

"You put a spell on me!" she gasped.

"No, I didn't!" Rose snapped back. "You were gripping it so tightly I'm surprised it didn't break into splinters! It wasn't even a chipped one," she said disgustedly, looking at the mess.

Mrs. Jones looked for a second as though her sympathies were with Rose, but then she shook her head. "Sarah, sweep it up, and do stop howling. You...do whatever it is you're meant to be doing."

She can't even use my name, Rose realized sadly.

"Did *she* do that?"

Rose leaped up from her chair and wheeled round to see Susan behind her with a tray of toast crusts and splashed milk—Isabella's afternoon tea. If it hadn't been for her lesson, she would have been the one fetching it. Despite Susan's declaration, she had ended up doing some of Rose's work.

"No!" she snarled and glared back at Susan.

"Freak," Susan hissed. "Witch girl. What was that witch doing with all those children in her cellar? Eating them? I wouldn't be surprised. That's what witches do. You'll start wanting to do that soon, I shouldn't wonder. Someone should get rid of you before you turn. One of my friends who works for a lord, she said I should look for a new place, instead of staying with murderers. You ought to be shut away, all of you."

Susan's accusation was unfortunately close to the truth. Mr. Fountain had been right, Rose realized. Gossip was flying round the city, and tempers were rising. *The snow won't help*, Rose thought suddenly. *Even I thought it was unnatural this early in the year. When children start dying of cold in the back alleys, they'll want someone to blame...*She blinked. *Maybe it is magical,* she thought suddenly. *But why would anyone waste magic making it snow?*

Susan sensed that Rose was no longer paying attention and took a threatening step forward.

Rose looked up and glared back at the older girl, her fingers itching. Why didn't she do something to Susan? She could. They hated her anyway, so it wouldn't make any difference. She deserved it. Rose watched a faintly wary expression settle in Susan's black eyes, and the older girl put the tray down slowly.

"Go on then," she said very quietly. "Show us what you can do. What are they teaching you?" She put her hands on her hips and walked slowly toward Rose. She was only a little taller, but she still managed to loom over the younger girl. Rose guessed Susan was depending on her being too overawed to do anything. She wasn't, she promised herself. She was scared of hurting Susan, that was all. Really.

She backed away, fumbling for the door, and ran. All the way up to her room in the attics, arriving in her own tiny space breathless and gasping. And furious, but mostly with herself, not Susan. *She* was just a mean, jealous, ugly, horrible toad, that was all. It was Rose who was stupid. She was going to have to do something; that was clear. Even the glory of magic lessons wasn't enough to make life worth living, when all but an hour of her day would be spent with people who hated her.

"And I hate *her*," she muttered miserably. "She's mean. Why does Susan have to be like this?" But what would *she* be like, Rose wondered, if a new girl had turned up, younger, everyone's pet—for Rose had been Mrs. Jones's favorite until the magic happened. Rose hoped she wouldn't have been quite as unpleasant as Susan, but she had to admit she would have been tempted to make a few catty remarks. And then Susan had discovered that the little maid from the orphanage, the one she'd been bossing about all over the place, could do things she would never be able to do. That one day Rose might even own a house like this. It would be hard to accept. It made sense. But that didn't make it any easier for Rose to put up with.

"And I won't," she said firmly. "Next time, I will do something horrible to her, and I don't care what they think." She sighed. Susan couldn't do it back though. Didn't that make winning a bit less special? A bit—easy?

A slow smile spread across her face. It didn't necessarily have to be something magical. There were plenty of things she could do to Susan without the merest hint of magic. Especially now she had access to the workroom, with its jars and cabinets full of interestingly scary spell ingredients. *Newts' eyes in Susan's porridge*, she thought dreamily. *The stuffed crocodile in her bed.* Rose giggled appreciatively at the thought.

* * *

She climbed the stairs to the workroom deliberately early the next day. None of the servants would complain if she said she was on her way to her lesson with Mr. Fountain—they might not like what their master did, but they had the utmost respect for his authority. Although even Miss Bridges had given Rose a horribly thoughtful look that morning. Rose had seen her glancing over Mrs. Jones's shoulder at the newspaper.

Rose had dithered over clearing the kitchen table, purposefully brushing against Mrs. Jones's arm as she moved the teacups. It hurt to see the woman who'd once bought her sweets hurry into the scullery to scrub away the touch of her skin, but it got her what she wanted. She skimmed the dense print hurriedly.

PARLIAMENT TO PASS LAW ON WITCHES

Rose's stomach kicked, and she tasted acid in her mouth. A law saying what? She read on, feeling sick. It seemed the headline was exaggerating somewhat, but there was to be a debate on whether "certain restrictions" should be made and licenses issued. Rose scowled at the paper—she wasn't sure what that meant, but it sounded bad. She looked up to find Mrs. Jones staring at her from the scullery door, a frightened look in her eyes.

Rose shook her head wearily. "I'm just the same as I was before," she told the cook, her voice shaking slightly. "I haven't changed."

Mrs. Jones nodded, but Rose knew she was only doing it so that the witch would leave. Rose whisked out of the kitchen, furious at the injustice of it all. All she had ever done was try to help!

Once in the workroom, she looked around carefully for Gus. He divided his time between this room and Mr. Fountain's study, with occasional forays to the kitchen for treats. She checked his usual sleeping places: the windowsill, on the chairs, under the table, sprawled on the back of the stuffed crocodile—he said its scales were good at scratching his itchy spine—but he was nowhere to be found. She huffed a little sigh of relief. She didn't want to explain this to him. Not so much because he would disapprove of her stealing from the workroom—he was more likely to ask why she was bothering, why she didn't just shrink Susan to the size of a pin and throw her in a gutter. He disapproved of Rose's cautious ways and wanted her to be more adventurous with her powers. Rose suspected he was as much of a dramatist as his master.

Rose wasn't quite sure what she was actually looking for. She wanted something disgusting probably, she thought. Something to scare Susan into leaving her alone. Spiders? It would work but, unfortunately, Rose didn't like them either. The thought of plunging her fingers into the jar labeled *Arachnids, dried, legs of* made her feel sick.

Cautiously, she stood on tiptoe to examine the cabinet that took up most of one wall. It was made of heavy, dark wood and contained hundreds of little drawers with brass mountings for slipping labels into. They were all marked in a variety of hands: a clear, flowing script she recognized as Mr. Fountain's, and Freddie's writing, less confident, with bits crossed out. But there were other hands too, and one who wrote in emerald-green ink that had never faded. The expert glamour-maker, Rose realized, wondering what he had used powdered rose quartz for. How many magicians had kept their secrets in this cabinet? It was possible that even Mr. Fountain didn't know everything that was in here. There had to be something she could use to have her revenge on Susan.

Rose started by carefully opening a few of the lower drawers. Most of them were full of strange powders and dusts. She had no idea what they all were, and she was reluctant to touch them. What if they were poison? She knew that one of the spells in *Prendergast's Perfect Primer*, the book that she and Freddie were supposed to be learning from, called for the dried venom of the Indian cobra. Any of these could be it.

She looked hopelessly up at the rows of drawers above her. She wondered miserably what on earth she thought she was going to find—and what would she do with it when she'd found it.

She sat down on the floor, unconscious for once of what she was doing to her dress. There had to be something—something to show Susan that Rose could fight back. Maybe just a little bit of magic wouldn't be cheating? Rose smiled grimly. Susan didn't have a problem taking advantage of her natural nastiness, after all.

Rose hopped up again and went to the big wooden table to leaf through *Prendergast*—that was how Freddie always referred to it. The book had a bossy, nanny-ish tone, but it was quite comforting at the same time. There were a few more advanced works on a shelf by the door, and even their covers looked frightening. One of them was bound in snakeskin, and Rose had heard it hiss. For now she would happily stick with the basic spells. She flicked through the heavy pages, her eyes drawn by a word here and there, glancing at the illustrations. What would upset Susan most?

She was incredibly vain, Rose thought to herself. She loved her clothes and hated her black uniform dresses. She'd saved her wages for a Sunday hat with violets on it. Rose squeaked, remembering, and leafed back. Yes, here it was. A Spell to Enliven an Image. It ought to work on velvet violets—they were a sort of image, weren't they?

Quickly, Rose dipped a scratchy pen into the inkwell and scribbled down the spell—it didn't seem too difficult, and all she needed was to burn a little piece of the image while she spoke the spell…

Ah. So she was going to have to steal a piece of Susan's Sunday hat. Rose nibbled one of her fingernails thoughtfully.

* * *

After the lesson, Rose hovered in the corridor, flicking a feather duster around and trying to look busy until Mr. Fountain had gone. Freddie and Gus stayed in the workroom, or so she thought.

She scuttled quickly to the attic stairs, which led up from this floor to the servants' bedrooms. It seemed unlikely that Susan would come upstairs in the afternoon, but it wasn't impossible.

"What are you doing?"

Rose stumbled and grabbed the banister to stop herself from falling. "Gus!"

The white cat was sitting on a step above her—which was impossible because he'd certainly been in the workroom when she'd left, and he hadn't gone past her. Rose wondered for a second if he could make himself invisible…

"You just don't look," Gus told her loftily, seeing her frown.

"What are you doing up here?" Rose demanded.

"I asked first." Gus stared down at her sternly.

Rose looked sideways. "I'm just fetching something…"

"Mmmm?"

"It isn't important." But Rose could feel how unconvincing she sounded. She sat down on the step below Gus. "How did you know?"

"You look excited. And frightened." He leaned down to rub his head against her ear. "Is it exciting?"

Rose laughed abruptly. "It's probably dangerous. I was going to steal a bit of one of the violets off Susan's Sunday hat, so I can make it so she's got a flowerpot on her head instead. I don't know if it would have worked. I just wanted to do *something*."

Gus sprang up, his tail twitching with excitement. "Come on!"

"You don't want to stop me?" Rose asked, almost hoping he would.

"Of course not. It's about time you showed that little madam what's what." Gus led the way up the stairs, his tail waving eagerly.

Susan's hat was hanging on a hook in her room, a room that was exactly like Rose's. Rose hovered in the doorway, holding the doorknob and not quite daring to let go.

"Oh, come on," Gus mewed irritably, and he darted in, leaping onto the bed and from there making a spectacular sideways leap, batting the hat off its hook with one gracefully outstretched paw. Then he picked it up in his teeth and trotted back to Rose, holding it like a large and flowery purple rat.

"Whatever does she put on her hair?" he muttered, spitting it out at Rose's feet. "Ugh. Do you have anything to cut a bit off with?"

Rose pulled a little knife out of her apron pocket. She'd borrowed it from the workroom, where it was used for cutting up roots and things, but now she looked at it rather doubtfully.

"Useless," Gus pronounced. "I do hope you're grateful, Rose. This whole revolting object is permeated with some foul hair oil." With his eyes closed in disgust, he quickly bit off one petal, and spat it into Rose's hand, furiously scrubbing at his mouth with a paw afterward. "Now what do we do?" he asked in a rather muffled voice.

"We get out of here," Rose muttered, beckoning him away and tucking the velvet petal away with the knife.

She was so nervous, she didn't think to put the hat back on its hook.

* * *

Rose was sitting in the back kitchen sewing, mending a hole in a sheet, while Bill polished shoes opposite her when Susan stormed in.

"Have you been in my room?" she snarled.

Caught out, Rose gaped at her, suddenly unable to think of anything to say. Across the table, Bill paused, holding a polishing rag in midair. "Don't talk daft," he muttered. "Why would she?" But he cast a slightly anxious glance at Rose.

Rose swallowed, her mouth tasting bitter. She didn't know whether to lie or not. She had wanted a showdown with Susan, after all.

It was just that she had wanted to be a little more prepared for it.

She pushed her chair back with a screech and stood

up. "All right. Yes, I went in your room." She pulled the tiny piece of purple velvet out of her apron pocket. "And I cut this off your hat." She decided not to implicate Gus. He might well be able to take care of himself, but Susan was sly enough to poison him. Rose wasn't going to risk it.

"You little brat! Little witch brat, you've done it now." Susan stepped forward, snatching the velvet scrap and seizing Rose's arm. "I'll make you wish you'd never been born."

Rose twisted, but Susan's fingers felt like iron bands.

"Let go of her," Bill demanded, surging around the table.

"What if I don't?" Susan sneered. "Going to pull me off her, are you? Get yourself in trouble for hitting a girl?"

Bill hesitated. It was true that if Susan said he'd hurt her, he would be in trouble, whatever excuse he came up with, even if it were true. Then he gulped, his eyes moving to Susan's hand, where it was clutching Rose's arm. Her nails were black. The dead color was spreading slowly up her fingers, seeping under the cuff of her dress.

Susan screamed and dropped Rose's arm, backing away, cradling her hand and moaning with horror.

"What did you do?" she whimpered. "You've poisoned me, haven't you, you little witch? I'm going to die."

"It'll stop now you've let go of me," Rose told her. *I hope*, she added to herself, crossing her fingers behind her back. She hadn't done the magic on purpose; it had been like the treacle-y horse, and all the other spells she'd done before she'd even known what she was. It had just…happened. But the dark stain faded gradually from Susan's fingers, leaving her hand a bloodless white.

It was the first time Susan had seen Rose do any magic. She stared at her, horror and disgust etched across her face. "Get away from me," she whispered. "You were going to kill me. You went in my room. What did you take? What did you leave there?"

"Nothing!" Rose insisted. "I was just going to do something to your stupid hat, that was all. To get you to leave me alone. And I wasn't trying to kill you. I only did that to your arm to make you let me go! You treat me like dirt, and you've no need." She stood up straighter and tried to sound brave, though she was as shaken as the other girl. "That was to show you. I can do it, and I will if you don't let me be. So."

But as she watched Susan backing out of the room, her eyes round and dark and fixed on Rose's face, she felt that it hadn't worked the way she wanted. Susan was terrified. She really believed Rose had been trying to attack her, maybe even kill her.

Rose realized miserably that she had been hoping for some amazing turnaround—that Susan would see her magic, and suddenly decide not to be mean anymore. Mrs. Jones and Sarah would come around as well, all laughing at Susan wearing a flowerpot on her head. Susan would be cross, but she'd realize that Rose wasn't to be trifled with. Everything would go back to the way it had been before, when Susan had been only bearably awful. The frightening newspaper articles Mrs. Jones loved to read would be about gory murders again, not magicians poisoning the world for everyone else.

It had been a dream, that was all. In real life, dreams hardly ever came true.

Five

ROSE SAT CURLED UP in her bed, her blankets heaped around her. She had lain awake for ages, too cold to sleep, until eventually she'd crept downstairs to one of the spare rooms and borrowed a silken quilt. It was probably something she could be dismissed for doing, but she almost didn't care anymore. Although of course, if she lost her job, she would be outside in the cold…

If she'd been back at St. Bridget's, they would all have squashed up two or three to a bed, just to keep warm, she thought, shivering still. She wished Gus would come and curl up with her, but he was probably sleeping with Freddie—the family's bedrooms would be much warmer. Perhaps she could go next door to Susan and ask if she'd like to share. Rose giggled bitterly. She stared into her candle flame, gazing at the blue heart of the fire. It blackened, slowly, like Susan's fingers, and Rose shuddered.

What was she going to do? Susan was never going

to forget about it now. She would take her revenge in small things, things Rose couldn't pin down. Even if Susan did nothing, Rose didn't think she could stand being looked at that way all the time—like a murderess. Miserably, she blew out the candle, watching the wick glow as the heat faded, until finally all was black. Then she wriggled further into her feathery nest. Pulling the quilt over her head shut everything else out. Rose wished she could stay there forever.

But the morning came all too quickly, and Rose woke, feeling confused. Something was different. It was still dark and piercingly cold, and for a moment she wondered if she'd woken too early. She had no clock in her room, of course, so she couldn't check, but it felt like her normal waking time of six. She lit her candle and held it up to the window, blinking in surprise to see the crystalline snow piled halfway up. She could just make out the whirling flakes—pretty, delicate, and unstoppable against the indigo sky.

Rose wrapped the stolen quilt around her shoulders and scrambled over her bed to her washing bowl. She had brought up a fresh jug of water the previous night, but it had frozen solid. No wonder she felt cold. The snow that Freddie had been so excited about two days ago had hardly lasted, but this looked as though it could set in for a while.

Rose scowled at the heavy, sugary snow piled against her window. It shouldn't be there, not in October.

This was depths-of-winter weather. It was wrong. The snow sparkled in a sudden flash of sunlight, and Rose shivered. The icy crystals shimmered, with that strange eye-straining effect that magic gave so much of the furniture in the Fountain house. They looked sharp and dangerous, and Rose wondered how frozen water could seem so wicked.

Rose tunneled her way out of the quilt and started to dress quickly, putting on both of the woolen vests that had been provided as part of her uniform and a red flannel petticoat. It meant she could hardly breathe once she'd done up her dress buttons, but she didn't care. She would wash in the kitchen. Hopefully the pump wouldn't be frozen too.

She scurried down the stairs, hoping to get in and out with her fire-lighting tray, preferably without seeing anyone, except maybe Bill. He would probably be rude to her, but there were acres of difference between Bill being rude and Susan being deliberately cruel. Bill was rude to everybody, except Miss Bridges.

She lingered over Miss Anstruther's fire after she'd lit it, warming her numb hands—the governess was still fast asleep and didn't even stir. Eventually Rose had to drag herself away, her fingers still feeling swollen and puffy as she tried silently to pick up her lucifer matches and sweeping brush.

Freddie was kneeling up on his windowsill, having hauled a quilt, much like the one Rose had borrowed, off his bed. It had a rich Eastern pattern, and he looked like a little blond sultan perched on the sill. "Look at it, Rose! This is going to stay for weeks!" he said hopefully. "A few hard frosts and we'll be sledding easily."

"You will, you mean," Rose told him, but she wasn't cross. Sometimes she felt years older than Freddie, even though she was almost certainly younger than he was.

"I wonder if one could skate on the fountain bowl in the park," Freddie replied dreamily. "Too small, maybe. Did you say something, Rose?"

Rose clanged the fire irons. "No," she told him shortly. It would be so nice to be rich, she thought darkly, and never have to worry about anything, except whether the snow would stick enough for sledding. She grinned ruefully to herself. She had a job, and this amazing magical gift that had come out of nowhere. What would she be wanting next, a palace?

"Are you all right?" Freddie asked, peering at her out of his cocoon of coverlets. "You look quite demented, sitting there grinning like that. Good servants don't show their emotions, Rose, you know. Not that you could be expected to know that sort of thing, considering your background," he added kindly, making Rose want to hit him.

"Thank you, sir," Rose murmured, trying to sound like a perfect servant.

Freddie gave her a suspicious look, but he was still half engrossed in watching the snow.

"Speaking as someone who'll have to help wash it, please don't get that coverlet dirty," Rose added as she closed the door behind her. She couldn't be a perfect servant all the time.

Down in the kitchens, Susan wouldn't meet her eyes. But Rose could feel her staring as soon as Rose wasn't watching her directly. It was a malevolent stare, hateful, and it prickled her skin. Rose told herself to ignore it. *I'm warm—almost. I have a job. I have food—* albeit a rather small portion of porridge, as she was clearly not Mrs. Jones's pet anymore—*Bill and Freddie and Bella talk to me. It doesn't matter.*

But as Susan passed on her way out, Rose felt a sharp tug at her head and turned to find Susan looking at her, wide-eyed with a mixture of triumph and fear, a dark hair pinched between her fingertips. "I've got a piece of you now," she whispered frantically. "You can't get me. We'll be rid of you, you'll see!"

Rose automatically turned to Mrs. Jones to protest, but the cook was looking abstractedly out of the window at the street above. She was humming too, which she never did.

"Ignore her, she's cracked," Bill muttered, but he looked rather spooked.

Rose shook her head, trying to think clearly. Did a hair mean anything? She didn't think so, but then she still knew almost nothing about magic. Maybe this was some powerful folklore, which she'd missed out on at

St. Bridget's. She tried to think it out as she climbed the stairs with a pile of fresh sheets, rubbing her eyes wearily. Her scalp stung.

Even if the hair pulling was nonsense, like Mrs. Jones's amulet, Rose wasn't sure how much more she wanted to put up with.

Maybe she didn't need to be an apprentice, she thought. She could teach herself, couldn't she? Her beloved, coveted job was turning to dust and ashes in front of her, but they couldn't take the magic away. She could use it, somehow, to survive.

She could find things! Like she'd found Maisie in Miss Sparrow's cellar. People always wanted lost things found. She'd start small but maybe one day have a little shop, where people came to see her, and she found their mislaid rings or stolen children or long-lost loves. Rose made Freddie's bed, dreamily furnishing her own tiny house above the shop. A little yard, with a rosebush in a pot. A yellow one.

She would miss Freddie, she thought, as she smoothed the Eastern coverlet, and Bill. But once she had earned enough money, they'd understand she didn't need to be dragged back, and she could go and see them. She would have to take her clothes, but she would earn the money to pay for them. Rose caught herself daydreaming again and told herself sternly not to be so stupid. There would be no houses with roses, not for a long while. It might take her years just to save the money to pay back her outfit. But it seemed better than this—this constant waiting for someone to pounce.

They wanted her gone. So she would go.

* * *

Rose thought about leaving all day, while she finished making the beds and moved on to sweeping and dusting all the upstairs rooms. Mrs. Jones sent her out to the grocer's just before lunch, as Mr. Fountain was lunching at home and had expressed a vague desire for Lancashire cheese. The extreme coldness of the snow brought Rose down to earth a little. She did not want to be out in it for any longer than she had to be, still less to be caught out in it without a home to return to. The snow was beautiful—though it was already turning brown with footsteps and carriage ruts. Where it was still clean, it glittered and sparkled like dry powder, so much so that Rose was tempted to remove her glove and sweep her fingers through it as it lay along the flat top of a stone wall. The glittery powder was only an illusion, and Rose cursed herself for being taken in as she blew on her scarlet fingers. Snow, she knew quite well, was wet, cold, and insidious. It got everywhere, and it was already getting into her boots. She hurried on to the grocer's, huddling in her hooded cloak and wishing for dry stockings. How could Freddie be so excited about this horrible, damp stuff?

But even the snow could not put her off the idea of leaving the house entirely, now that the thought had taken hold. She couldn't concentrate on the lesson that afternoon, and her glamour hardly worked at all, merely growing her fingernails to the size of claws. She was hardly listening when Mr. Fountain dismissed Freddie but asked her to wait behind. Rose expected that he had special instructions about the cleaning of the workroom or a message for Miss Bridges, but after Freddie closed the door, Mr. Fountain merely gazed at her, his gray eyes dark with worry.

"What is it, sir?" Rose asked, somehow sure that he knew what she was planning. Once before he had seemed to read her mind, and why else would he stare at her so?

"No, Rose. I can't read minds—or only to the most elementary level. But I watch faces, and your face has your story written on it like a book." Mr. Fountain sighed. "What are you planning to do when you leave?"

Rose gaped at him. How could he say he couldn't read minds? How did he know? "I'm sorry, sir," she whispered. "I don't mean to be ungrateful."

"Are we making it so very hard for you?" Mr. Fountain asked her, pacing up and down the room in his agitation. "I had thought you quite enjoyed these lessons. Freddie has not been showing his jealousy, has he?"

Rose shook her head frantically, her short hair

flailing in a way Miss Bridges would have called most unladylike. "Oh, no! I mean, he hasn't, and I do, very much. It isn't that…" She hung her head miserably.

"Someone else, then." Mr. Fountain stared at her thoughtfully. "The other servants. I should have thought about that. Of course they wouldn't be happy about you being elevated to an apprentice. The other maids are jealous?"

"They're not jealous! They hate me!" Rose shook her head in disbelief. "You don't understand, do you? They're terrified of me because they think I'm going to kill them. Susan pulled a hair out of my head because she says it means I can't kill her now!"

"Well, it depends what she's planning to do with it…" Mr. Fountain murmured. "I would have thought it most unlikely that she had the necessary skill…"

Rose scowled at him. Then she remembered he was her employer and quickly folded her hands on the front of her apron and stared at them, her face politely blank.

"Oh, don't do that. It's incredibly irritating," Mr. Fountain muttered. "I'm sorry, Rose. Are they really so scared? They're my servants, after all. What do they think pays their wages?"

"Gold." Gus spoke from the windowsill, where he was gazing out at the snow. "It's all that keeps them here."

Mr. Fountain looked unhappy. "I thought we had gone some way past this ridiculous suspicion of magic.

At least in this house, surely. Whatever the rest of the world thinks…"

"But you *could* kill them all if you wanted to." Gus shrugged, a full-body cat shrug that was very expressive. "They're right to be scared."

"I wouldn't though," Mr. Fountain complained.

"Miss Sparrow would," Rose said quietly. "And there might be others. Unless all magicians are law-abiding and trustworthy and perfect, shouldn't everyone else be scared?"

Mr. Fountain looked uncomfortable. "Well, perhaps… But the brotherhood of magicians is most honorable. We use our skills for the benefit of all. We don't attempt to seize power or rule others in any way."

Gus made a noise that sounded like *Hmf.*

"Well, not often…or only when necessary…" Mr. Fountain caught Rose's expression and sighed.

"What exactly were you intending to do, Rose? You haven't answered my question."

"I thought I could find things for people," Rose said very quietly. She was expecting them to belittle her, tell her that her talent wasn't strong enough. She sat down at the table again, staring at the scratches and stains that patterned its surface. "I suppose it wouldn't work…"

Instead, Mr. Fountain leaned against the table and rubbed his hands over his eyes wearily, and Gus leaped down from the windowsill to weave lovingly around his legs.

"Of course it would," Mr. Fountain sighed. "You would be wonderful at it." He looked up at her. "Don't you see? You're too good, Rose. Setting aside that it would be a complete waste of your powers, you are *too good*. You would be able to find anything anyone wanted."

Rose stared at him, puzzled. "But…what's wrong with that? Isn't it good to help people who've lost something? I mean, I know it's sad that I would have to get them to pay me, but I wouldn't charge very much."

Mr. Fountain laughed harshly, almost bitterly, and Gus jumped into Rose's lap. "Silly child," he told her in an affectionate purr.

Rose looked at them, hurt, and Mr. Fountain sighed.

"I shouldn't laugh at you, Rose. Such innocence should be refreshing."

Rose began to feel as though she must have said something very stupid. Her eyes burned. The servants hated her, and she didn't understand magicians properly either. She belonged nowhere.

"You've upset her," Gus told Mr. Fountain. He looked at her interestedly, with his head on one side and his ears perked up. "Look, you see, now, if she were a cat, she would be washing. Humans are most handicapped by not being able to wash without added water. It's such a useful distraction in this kind ation." He stood up and put his paws on Rose' ders, nosing her affectionately.

55

"Oh, do be quiet," Mr. Fountain muttered. "Rose, I'm not trying to be unkind. I just need you to understand. You cannot go out into the streets of London and set yourself up as a finder. Oh, yes, there are such people. Those who have the merest ghost of a talent and a little luck, and they scrape themselves a living—"

"So why can't I?" Rose burst out angrily, turning her face away from Gus's tickling whiskers.

"You'd last a fortnight..." Gus purred in her ear.

Rose stroked him without meaning to, running her hand down his smooth side and admiring the soft fringe of longer fur round his rather large stomach. Then she dropped her hand and scowled.

"Stop it! You're glamouring me, aren't you? It isn't fair!"

Gus reeled back from her, his ears laid flat and his luxuriant whiskers drooping dejectedly. Rose blinked. She'd been angry, but she hadn't meant to upset him so.

"I'm sorry—don't look so upset..." she murmured apologetically.

Gus's whiskers sprang back to their usual jaunty angle and he purred with satisfaction. "Got you that time!"

"Oh!" Rose hissed crossly through her teeth. "You shocking liar!"

"What Gustavus is trying to explain to you," Mr.

Fountain glared at his cat, "is that you would actually find things."

Rose nodded, not understanding. "I might even be good at it," she pleaded.

"Rose, the police employed a finder to look for Emmeline Chambers after Miss Sparrow stole her. It was at the request of her parents when no progress had been made in the case—they even paid the exorbitant fee. The man found nothing—or rather, he swore that Emmeline had been taken to Paris by a man on a black horse."

"But that's nonsense," Rose said slowly.

"Of course. And that man makes a very good living by peddling nonsense." Mr. Fountain twirled the end of his mustache. "If you go out there and show people like that your talent, Rose, you'll be back in a cellar in—I disagree with Gus here—much less than a fortnight."

"More likely in pieces in a succession of sacks floating down the Thames," Gus purred ghoulishly.

"You're probably right. Rose, you would put them all to shame. Someone with an inferior talent would get rid of you. Or some unscrupulous person would decide to take you under their 'protection.' Purely for your own safety, of course."

"And then how long do you think it would be before you were finding things that weren't lost in the first place?" Gus stared into Rose's eyes, his own parti-colored ones deeply serious.

"If you were shown a picture of a jewel case, Rose, do you think you could find where in a house it might be hidden?" Mr. Fountain asked her.

"I suppose so…" Rose whispered miserably. She could see that they were right. She would never be able to reveal what she could do.

Another dream was gone.

"Don't look like that, Rose," Mr. Fountain told her gently.

"But if I can't let anyone know that I can find things, or see pictures, what am I going to do?" Rose asked. "I thought I'd be happy being a maid. I'd always known I wanted to have a job and earn my own living. But…I don't think I could go back to only that now. And I can't get rid of my magic anyway, I tried."

Mr. Fountain smiled. "I'm not saying you should give up. Just stick it out for a couple more years, Rose. When you're trained enough to control your power properly, to protect yourself, then you can go anywhere, do anything, be anyone you like."

"But for now, you need to stay where we can protect you," Gus agreed.

Rose gave him a slightly old-fashioned look, as though wondering how much protection a middle-sized white cat was going to provide, and Gus glared back, shook his whiskers, and suddenly there was a Bengal tiger sitting on Rose's lap. She nearly fell over backward, and Gus downshifted again.

"Sorry," Rose muttered, stretching her legs to see if they felt broken. She decided Gus must have taken on the tiger glamour without actually making himself all that heavy, but it still felt as though she ought to be squashed. "I see what you mean."

"Good," Gus said sniffily. "After all my help with Miss Sparrow, no more demeaning glances, please. A white cat is a very useful form to keep to. Attractive, unthreatening, and I have my own integral defenses." He ran a claw sharply into Rose's leg to demonstrate, and she winced but didn't say anything.

"Don't maul her, Gus," Mr. Fountain said. He was looking thoughtfully at Rose, a gaze that made her feel uncomfortable, as though it was rubbing away the surface of her skin.

"What is it, sir?" she asked defensively.

"I was just wondering about you, Rose. I've been wondering for a while, to tell the truth, where you could have come from."

"I came from the orphanage," Rose told him, her face obstinately set.

Mr. Fountain frowned at her, and she wriggled on her chair.

"You know quite well what I mean," he told her gently. There was a firmness in his voice that she usually heard him use with Freddie when he was being particularly dim. Rose thought that Freddie was being dim on purpose quite a lot of the time, and she had a feeling he was doing it more since she'd come along. It wasn't that he didn't like her, but he didn't like her showing him up. If he wasn't going to be as good as Rose, he was going to be not as good his way. So she reckoned, anyway. She was trying to be sympathetic, but the temptation to clip him around the earhole was growing by the day. She had a feeling Mr. Fountain felt the same way about his first apprentice. Gus certainly did, and Freddie had a nice collection of scratch patterns on his hands from annoying Gus too much. The cat wasn't known for his patience.

"Your parents must have known," Mr. Fountain muttered. "So why leave you?" He shook his head. "Something must have happened to them. You must have been left with someone who didn't understand. That's all I can think."

Rose shivered and hoped they didn't notice. She couldn't help remembering what Susan had called her. A changeling. It sounded much the same as what the master was saying now.

"Would I have been—strange?" she asked with difficulty. "I mean, would people have been able to tell?" There had been nothing odd noted in her records at St. Bridget's.

Mr. Fountain shook his head. "Not necessarily. I mean, some small children can show signs early, but it's more usual at around your age. Freddie manifested his powers particularly early—he was only seven—which is why it's so damned annoying that the boy won't apply himself now." He blinked and bowed to her slightly. "I do apologize. Most unfortunate language. Idiot boy provokes me." He shuddered. "I expect my daughter's magic will start to show soon. We will need to find her a somewhat more hard-wearing governess." Rose giggled. Miss Anstruther was definitely on the delicate side. But then, anyone would be, shut up with Isabella all day. Rose had already seen the little girl grow claws in a temper. She wouldn't put it past Bella to hide whatever magic she was growing until just when she wanted it.

"Which reminds me, I must speak to Isabella. Will you send her to my study, Rose, please?" He smiled at her hopefully. "You will stay, won't you? I can't let you go. It would be like throwing you to the wolves. Freddie and I have a responsibility for you now, until you're grown. Don't you realize that? Our magic binds us together, a shared heritage—even if we don't know where we inherited it."

Rose dropped her eyes, not wanting him to see her tears. It sounded as though he was calling her family.

Six

R OSE TOOK HER TIME going to the schoolroom to fetch Bella. Mr. Fountain wouldn't notice. It was well-known in the household that he lived in a dream world half the day, shut away in his study. One had to catch him at the right time. Bella was possibly the only person who could snap him back to reality whenever she wanted to.

Rose hid herself in one of the window alcoves on the corridor, ducking behind a table bearing a large pottery horse. Rose rather liked it, as it was more battered than a lot of the ornaments in the house. The rider had been knocked about a bit, and the horse was dark brown, with odd greenish splotches on him. It seemed as though it had been decorated by someone who'd gotten bored and decided just to flick a brush at it. But for all that, it looked very like a horse, although one with a rather big bottom. Rose stroked it gently and leaned her head on her arms, staring at the horse's hooves.

Isabella could have the same skin-scrubbing effect as

her father, and if Rose went to the schoolroom now, Bella would have every last detail of Susan's insults and Rose's innermost feelings out of her. Rose wanted her innermost feelings to stay innermost, and Bella was an interfering little gossip who'd love to sneak down to the kitchen and wreak some horrible revenge on Rose's part—a revenge that would almost certainly backfire on Rose. So staring at the horse's smooth, brown legs to calm down for a few minutes was worth the risk of being caught idling.

Something nuzzled her hair, and Rose jumped, realizing her daydreams had slipped into real dreams. She looked around for Gus, assuming it was he who'd woken her, but he was nowhere to be seen. Rose blinked at the horse, which was staring off into the middle distance with the innocent expression of someone thinking the grass in the painting of the foolishly dressed shepherdess on the far wall looked quite delicious. The rider was grinning more than he had been too.

"Thank you," Rose murmured, sliding around the table. The horse flicked its odd little stub of a tail, just a smidge.

The schoolroom was ominously quiet. Bella was curled up in the window seat, clutching a large doll and looking both angelic and bored, which was a dangerous combination, particularly as she seemed quite delighted to see Rose.

"Where's Miss Anstruther?" Rose inquired, cautiously.

"Prostrate. Again. If Papa didn't pay her such

enormously high wages, she'd definitely have gone into a decline by now," Bella purred.

"What did you do?" Rose was intrigued. Bella was never short of ideas. Perhaps she could borrow something to use on Susan.

"Nothing."

"I don't believe you." Rose shook her head, but Bella smiled. She looked much less angelic smiling.

"Really. Absolutely nothing. That's what I did. Miss Anstruther's always saying *Sit still, Isabella*, and *Silence, Isabella*. So that's what I did. I was only doing what I was told," she added innocently.

Rose grinned. "Your father wants you."

Bella looked faintly worried. "How on earth did he *know*? Oh well. Perhaps it'll convince him that Miss Anstruther just isn't up to the task of educating me."

Rose shook her head. "I don't think he knew about you prostrating her again. He just wanted to see you about something. And I'll be back up with your tea in a minute, miss," she added.

"Oh, good, sitting still makes one dreadfully hungry. Can you make sure there's lots of cake?" Isabella disappeared in a whirl of lace petticoats, and Rose smoothed her apron, readying herself to go back belowstairs.

When she came back with the tea tray, which Sarah had refused to hand to her, putting it down on the kitchen table so Rose had to pick it up herself, Isabella hadn't returned.

Rose tidied the schoolroom, putting away the books and picking up Miss Anstruther's chair, which seemed to have been knocked over, perhaps as its owner ran out of the room.

She wondered if Isabella was having tea with her father, and she was just about to take the tray back downstairs when Bella stamped back in and slammed the door. Her golden ringlets were like springs, coiling out from her scalp and vibrating with crossness. Rose eyed the china nervously.

"I hate them!" Isabella snapped. "I hate them, and I can't say so, and I'll have to behave, and they're so idiotically *stupid*! It isn't fair!"

Rose wondered for a moment if Miss Anstruther had been replaced with a fleet of new governesses. "Who is?" she asked, daringly, considering she was so close to the teapot.

Isabella flounced over to the table and seized a biscuit, biting it viciously with small, white teeth.

"I have to go to tea at the palace tomorrow," she told Rose blackly.

"The palace?" Rose gasped. "The king's palace?"

"How many other palaces are there?" Bella snapped. "Of course the king's palace. I have to go and eat Bath buns with those perfect, sweet, deathly dull little princesses."

Rose's legs wobbled, and she sat down at the table and gazed at Bella, her mouth hanging open. "You're having tea with them?"

"Close your mouth, or I'll throw crumbs in it," Bella snarled. "You look like a fish."

"Princess Jane and Princess Charlotte?" Rose persisted, ignoring the warning signs. "Don't throw that at me!"

Bella had seized the plate of cake, and Rose wrestled it away from her. "I thought you were hungry," she said, waving it at Bella with considerable cunning. "You can't eat it if it's been on the floor, can you?"

Isabella sighed moodily and accepted a piece of currant cake. "Even the cake isn't as good as you'd expect from a palace," she muttered.

"Do you go there often?" Rose asked eagerly. She couldn't help it. The little princesses were fairy-tale characters, yet the whole country felt as though the girls belonged to them.

Princess Jane was nearly eight years old—the same age as Isabella. She had been born—most inconveniently, the royal family had thought at the time—on the eve of a great sea battle with Talis, a battle that the Admiralty had been rather expecting to lose. The Talish had been worryingly close to swarming across the Channel, and if their ships had destroyed the flower of the Royal Navy, as they had confidently expected to, they would have been followed by transports carrying an invasion.

Instead, the battle had turned into the most amazing victory, as the captain of the most strategically placed man-of-war had made a gallant speech to his men about fighting for their country and remembering that their beloved prince had a new baby daughter, who must not be allowed to be brought up Talish. It had been stirring stuff, and the salient points had been repeated to the other ships of the line using flags, which had made it somewhat shorter but still most affecting. After the Talish had been driven away in tatters, the ships had limped triumphantly home to port, and the navy had been given royal permission to rename the man-of-war, previously called the *Redoubtable*, which nobody liked very much, *Princess Jane*.

The little princess had become an unofficial mascot of the Royal Navy, and adoring sailors were always presenting her with pieces of furniture made from spare bits of ships. On one occasion a sailor had almost been dismissed from the service for borrowing a bulkhead to whittle a doll for the princess, who was visiting his ship. But she had admired the doll, and he had been raised to master's mate instead.

The battle had caused a dramatic change of heart in the Talish government. Because it had been such a disaster, the emperor had been forced to give up on the invasion plan, due to popular pressure, and a fragile peace had lasted ever since. It was very fragile though, and most people thought that the Talish were bound to try again eventually.

The navy now had another ship named *Princess*

Charlotte, and shortly after the new little princess had been born, her grandfather, the old king, had died. Prince Albert had become king, and the little princesses had played a large part in the coronation ceremony, embedding themselves deeper in the nation's hearts. Even the orphans at St. Bridget's had shared in the joy of the populace, as there had been cake, which was so rare as to be unforgettable.

So to Rose, the princesses were a source of cake and amazing stories. Princess Jane wore underwear entirely made of the finest lace, the orphans had said wisely, while laundering their plain drawers. Princess Charlotte had a little carriage drawn by two enormous wolfhounds, sent by the emperor of Russia, her father's cousin. Their older sisters, the princesses Sophia, Victoria, and Lucasta, only washed in water from golden bowls and occasionally had baths in milk. The orphans had not been quite sure about this, as it sounded rather smelly, although undeniably grand.

"I can't believe you don't want to go..." Rose sighed, staring at Isabella dreamily. "I'll go instead if you like..."

"Done. Get Gus to help you make a glamour," Bella snapped. "They're so awfully good, Rose. Even you would be bored. All Princess Jane talks about is her duty to the country. It's a great pity she'll never be queen—I mean, they can't possibly lose three older princesses. That would just be wasteful."

Rose looked at her thoughtfully. "I suppose you actually have to behave at the palace. It must be quite difficult."

Isabella stared at her icily. "Won't you have been missed in the kitchens?" she asked, her voice honeyed. "What are you going to tell them? That you were clearing up after I had another tantrum? Would you like me to throw the tea tray at the wall? I'd hate you to have to lie."

Rose got up very quickly and curtsied. "Have you quite finished, miss?" she asked, seizing the tray and holding it protectively.

Isabella sighed. "Let me have another piece of cake," she muttered gloomily. "I need to make up for tomorrow. Princess Jane actually *prefers* bread and butter."

Seven

ISABELLA DULY WENT TO tea the next day, in her best red velvet cloak with the sable around the hood. Rose watched her through one of the upstairs windows, which she was supposed to be washing. As Isabella climbed into the carriage, she looked like she was being taken to the palace to be executed, not to eat cake. Or even bread and butter.

Rose took Bella's supper up to the schoolroom later, wondering if she would get away without having the cocoa thrown at her.

Bella was grumpy but resigned. "Oh, Rose, not more bread and butter," she moaned, when she saw the tray.

"Don't tell," Rose murmured conspiratorially, drawing a piece of shortcake out of her apron pocket. "I don't think Mrs. Jones thought you'd want much after tea at the palace. Did they really only have bread and butter? No éclairs? No talking gingerbread men?"

"They have them," Bella explained. "The éclairs

at least. But I can't eat them unless the princesses do. And they don't. Maybe because they can have them all the time, but actually I think Jane just likes bread and butter." Bella shook her head. "Can you imagine turning down éclairs for bread and butter?"

Rose considered briefly. "No."

"Nor me," Bella sighed.

"Perhaps you won't have to go again for a while," Rose suggested.

Bella shook her head grimly. "No, I have to keep going. For some reason, Princess Jane finds me amusing, and she wants me to come to tea every week." She shrugged. "Papa says I must. It would be disadvantageous to his career to say no, not to mention mine, eventually. I wouldn't mind being a palace magician. And anyway, Papa says he wants me to be at the palace. There are a lot of horrible rumors going around about magicians and how they aren't to be trusted. He says me being friends with the princesses just now is diplomatically useful." She brightened a little. "I might ask him if you can come too, Rose! I promised Princess Jane I would bring Freddie next week, so he could show her some magic—they don't get to see an awful lot of it, and Freddie can do some things, even if he is a bit useless. I wouldn't feel so terribly dowdy if I had my own maid with me. I think they were quite surprised that I didn't." She frowned, her bottom lip sticking out. "I wish Papa would have more servants. I should like to have a proper lady's maid." She looked hopefully at Rose. "You would come, wouldn't you? I mean, you'd have to if I said so, but you would anyway?"

Rose nodded eagerly. Bella might be a brat, but Rose had a certain affection for her—and she would crawl behind the little girl on her knees if it meant going to see the palace.

* * *

Freddie was distinctly less keen when it was broken to him that he was going to the palace too.

"Oh, Bella, no!" he exclaimed in horror when she told him the next day. She was in the workroom, escaping Miss Anstruther and teasing Gus, who didn't like her. Bella had a piece of embroidery silk, which she was wafting in front of his nose. He might be a magical cat, but he still had all the usual cat instincts, and he was having to try very hard not to chase it. His eyes were fixed on the twitching thread, and his tail was flicking backward and forward in desperation.

"Oh, just chase it, Gus, you know you want to!" Freddie spat crossly. "Why do I have to go to the palace, Bella? I'll have to wear my best suit and that stupid lace collar."

"Princess Jane asked for you," Bella told him, oozing smugness. "You have to. Royal command."

Freddie muttered something unintelligible, but it obviously wasn't polite.

"I told her you were Raph's cousin, and she thinks Raph is wonderful, so she's looking forward to you coming." Bella giggled.

Freddie scowled. "Raph gets away with everything just because he's so handsome. It's deeply unfair."

"Princess Lucasta is absolutely in love with him," Bella confided. "She was there while we were having tea, talking to one of the ladies-in-waiting."

"Wonderful," Freddie muttered. "Now he's going to have an unsuitable romance with a princess. It's a disaster. She's going to marry some Russian tsarevich, everyone knows that! My whole family is going to be sent into exile tomorrow. Why can't Raph just—just keep his mouth shut?"

"I don't think he has to talk for people to fall in love with him, Freddie," Bella pointed out. "In fact, it's probably better if he doesn't; every time I've met him, he's talked the most complete nonsense. He's far better if he just shuts up and looks pretty."

Rose blinked at her. Sometimes it was hard to believe Isabella was only eight, but then she had had a rather unusual upbringing. She and her father were very close, and he liked to talk to her about everything.

"Well, I shall have to go then," Freddie agreed, "just to make sure Raph isn't about to do something stupid." He thought for a moment and corrected himself. "More stupid than usual."

* * *

As she climbed into the Fountains' carriage, Rose realized that she was the only person who actually wanted to be there. Miss Anstruther was shooing them all in, twittering anxiously about everyone being on their best behavior. Even Rose was ignoring her. She and the governess had to sit with their backs to the horses, of course, facing Isabella and Freddie, who were sitting in mutinous silence.

The coachman was distinctly grumpy too, and slammed the carriage door with a hand wearing at least three layers of unraveling fingerless gloves. There had been a new fall of snow in the night, and the roads were treacherous. Bill had already had to shovel a pathway clear around the front of the house, and he'd told Rose he thought bits of him might have fallen off, only he couldn't tell which because he was numb all over. The coach horses, beautiful grays called Apollo and Ares, looked quite depressed and kept pawing at the ground, as though they couldn't believe they were expected to go out in this weather.

Rose huddled herself into her cloak, grateful that it was so much thicker than the threadbare shawl she had brought from the orphanage. The news that she was going to the palace with Isabella had thrown the household into a flurry of sewing and carefully considered shopping. None of the dresses she already had, sensible cotton prints, or even her black wool dress for church, were deemed suitable for visiting royalty.

Rose stroked the new cloak lovingly as she gazed out of the carriage window. It was nothing compared to Bella's furs, of course. But it had been bought new, from a shop, and no one had worn it before her. It even had velvet ribbon, three rows, running around the bottom. Under it she had a new dress—not even a black one, but a soft dark-green wool, with neat little horn buttons. Mr. Fountain had told Miss Bridges that Rose should have her wages raised, as she was working as an apprentice as well as a maid, and he'd said she should have a dress that showed her new position too. And that morning, Rose had even been sent to the Pantheon Bazaar to buy herself a new pair of stockings. Altogether, it was most satisfactory. Susan's covetous looks at those rows of velvet ribbon were particularly gratifying.

"Isabella, I do hope you will not be showing that sulky face to their Royal Highnesses," Miss Anstruther pleaded. "You really must appear a little more pleased! And you, Master Frederick! We are not going to the dentist, after all!" She tittered anxiously at her own joke then sighed sadly as Bella and Freddie simply glared at her.

"I blame you for this entirely, Bella," Freddie muttered. "And *what* magic does Princess Jane want to see? I'm not a conjuror. I hope she doesn't think I'm going to pull rabbits out of hats or anything stupid like that."

"Can you not think of anything for yourself?" Bella scolded. "Honestly, you know what they're like. Just make something pretty happen!" She sighed. "Really, I could probably do it better myself." She looked down at her little velvet reticule thoughtfully, as though wondering what she could pull out of it.

"Isabella! What have you got in that bag?" Miss Anstruther asked anxiously.

"Just a handkerchief," Isabella told her sweetly, staring at her governess with wide blue eyes. The little velvet bag seemed to squirm.

Rose, sitting diagonally opposite Bella, could see quite well that Bella was wriggling her fingers underneath the reticule, but Miss Anstruther went white and started to make a strange gobbling noise, like a very sick chicken. Then she flopped back against the seat cushions and moaned.

"Oh, she's going to have the vapors again," Bella muttered disgustedly. "Really, it's just too easy. Rose, her smelling salts are in her bag."

Rose took Miss Anstruther's shabby black bag and felt around in it, drawing out a little glass stoppered bottle.

"I gave her that last Christmas," Bella observed, in a gratified sort of way. "I thought she might as well have a nice one, since I seem to make her use it so much."

Rose waved the aromatic salts under Miss Anstruther's nose, and she gasped.

"Do wake up, miss," Rose told her. "Miss Bella was just being silly. I should think we'll be there soon."

Indeed they were now traveling along Palace Hill, leading up to the amazing white building. Rose let the salts drop into Miss Anstruther's lap and stared. She had never seen it before—how would she? Mr. Fountain's house was in a less aristocratic area of the town, where many of London's rich merchants lived. Before she went into service, Rose had only seen the few streets between the orphanage and the church. The palace and the surrounding parks had been quite out of her way. The white palace, in the white snow, almost shone (if one ignored the smoky soot on the marble and the who-knows-what in the snow, which Rose could, just for a moment).

Miss Anstruther smiled. "I forgot you would not have seen it, Rose. Is it not beautiful? King Albert has had it redesigned, you know, since his accession. He felt his father's ideas were a little out of date, they say. A wonderful new ballroom, with fifteen crystal chandeliers!"

"Papa says it is a vulgar monstrosity," Bella observed, looking out her window with a rather bored expression.

"Isabella! I'm sure your dear papa said no such thing!" Miss Anstruther sounded quite shocked, and Bella shrugged.

"He doesn't like all the gilding. And he says the cherubs in the Gold Drawing Room are coy."

Miss Anstruther gazed at her, speechless, and even

Rose felt rather horrified. Was that sort of thing treason? she wondered. Could Bella and her father be imprisoned for saying that the new palace was tasteless?

"You don't say that sort of thing when you're actually *at* the palace, do you?" Rose asked, leaning forward while trying not to be too obvious. Miss Anstruther looked like someone had slapped her in the face with a fish, but she might come to her senses at any moment, and she would be bound to disapprove of Bella's maid being so forward.

Bella shook her head. "Oh, no. Or at least, I try very hard not to." She sighed. "Sometimes I just have to say something, or I'll burst. But luckily Princess Jane seems to think I'm being amusing—and Charlotte is too little to understand anyway."

Rose had stopped listening. "Oh my goodness…look at that enormous great arch. Do we go through there?"

"Of course not!" Freddie grinned at her, enjoying feeling superior. "Only the royal family can go through it. We'll go around to the Royal Mews at the side."

"Oh." Rose nodded. It didn't really matter. She had just wondered what it would be like to drive through the archway—it was the grandest thing she'd ever seen. A haughty-looking stone woman with a spear was staring down at her, clearly thinking that this brat was not going anywhere near her arch. "What happens if someone who isn't the royal family goes through it? What if, I don't know, my bonnet blew off and landed in the

78

middle of the archway? Would I be allowed to go and fetch it?"

"No," Bella said definitely.

Freddie looked thoughtful. "Well, the Riding Troop of the Horse Artillery can pass through it too, to guard the king, so I suppose you'd have to ask one of them to get it." Then he smirked. "I wonder who cleans up the horse droppings," he whispered, keeping a wary eye on Miss Anstruther, who was moaning slightly. "The Horse Guards are the ones in the shiny brass helmets and plumes. They're much too grand to do it. I bet it gets smelly in there."

Rose and Bella pretended to look shocked, but they were all still giggling as they drove up to the much less distinguished back entrance of the palace.

Mr. Fountain's coachman let down the carriage steps, and Rose got down first to help Bella and Miss Anstruther out.

Bella looked over at the door as she jumped down and frowned. "Why's no one waiting for us? Usually there's a page on the steps, waiting to take me up to the princesses' rooms." Bella looked quite put out. She had been looking forward to showing off to Rose, for the page would have recognized her and led her straight into the palace.

Instead of a page, two very large guardsmen with ceremonial pikes were standing one on either side of the door, their faces frozen.

"What do we do now?" Freddie hissed. The guardsmen looked almost twice as tall as he was.

"I don't know!" Bella muttered back. "Usually they just stay there like that. I always want to pinch them to see if they'll do anything."

"Don't!" Freddie yipped.

"Miss Anstruther!" Bella demanded.

Her governess was hunting through her bag distractedly and didn't seem to have noticed that they hadn't been met. "Yes, Isabella, dear?"

"What do we do? No one's here to meet us."

Everyone stared at Miss Anstruther. Rose thought that even one of the guards swiveled his eyes hopefully in her direction.

Miss Anstruther looked vague. "Oh…well, perhaps we should just go in—you know your way…"

Bella, Freddie, and Rose formed a neat line behind the governess, and Bella pushed her gently up the steps. At the top, Miss Anstruther reached out for the door handle and squeaked with dismay as the guardsmen's pikes slammed down in front of her. Clearly they were not so ceremonial after all.

"That's my governess! You can't spear my governess!" Bella squeaked indignantly. Only she was allowed to torture Miss Anstruther.

"No entry," one of the guards intoned flatly, but he did look rather worried. Disemboweling governesses probably did not form part of his usual duties.

Miss Anstruther chose that moment to keel over backward down the steps, most unfortunately flashing the guards with several lace-edged petticoats and her drawers. She also fell on Freddie and Rose.

"Oh, pick her up!" Bella snapped, stamping one little button-booted foot. Miss Anstruther had missed her, probably out of a well-developed sense of self-protection. "Yes, you! How dare you assault my governess? My father is the Chief Magical Counselor to the Treasury! He will turn you into coins!"

"Help!" Freddie moaned feebly. "Can't breathe!"

Rose wriggled out from underneath Miss Anstruther's stiff bombazine skirts and tried to tug the governess up again to rescue Freddie.

"Help us!" Bella smacked one of the guards in the leg and went to haul Miss Anstruther's other hand.

The soldiers exchanged worried glances and clearly decided that Bella was a more present danger than being court-martialed for abandoning their post. They stepped down to help pick up the dead weight of the collapsed governess.

"Better get her inside," one of them muttered. "Ask one of the stewards where to put her. Or get that idiot equerry that was hanging around."

"Raph again. Bound to be," Freddie wheezed, as Miss Anstruther was lifted off him.

"Yes, the equerry is his cousin. You'd better find him," Bella directed firmly.

The guards looked even more worried as they found that this gaggle of squashed children had important connections. One of them opened the door with a flourish, and the other dumped Miss Anstruther onto a spindly gold chair in the hallway.

Rose looked around. She was not impressed so far—surely a palace ought to be rather more organized than this? And she could hear shouting. One did not shout in a palace. Everything was supposed to be hushed and serene and beautiful. Or at least in the public apartments, anyway. She'd imagined it rather like a swan, perfect on the surface but kicking away like mad underneath.

A group of soldiers ran past, looking anxious, with their swords drawn, and Rose stared at Freddie and Bella.

"Is it usually like this?" she whispered worriedly.

"No," Freddie muttered. "I do hope we haven't chosen to visit in the middle of a revolution. This is all your fault, Bella!"

"No one came through this door?" A much more grandly dressed soldier strode up to the guards, who stopped fanning Miss Anstruther with their handkerchiefs and tried to look as though they hadn't just deserted their posts.

"No, sir!"

"Who are these?" The officer glared at the children, finally allowing his gaze to linger distastefully on Miss Anstruther, who whimpered slightly.

Bella was made of much sterner stuff. "I am Isabella Fountain, and my papa is going to be extremely annoyed when I tell him about this!" she retorted. "We are supposed to be going to tea with Princess Jane."

The officer stared blankly at her, then gave a short bark of laughter. "You find her, my dear, and you can have as much tea as you want." Wearily he rubbed a gloved hand, encrusted with gold braid, across his face.

Everyone stared at him.

"You've lost the princess?" Freddie whispered in horror.

The soldier went white, as he realized what he'd done. "Certainly not," he snapped. "And anyone spreading rumors to that effect will be guilty of incitement and revolution and other...very bad things." He glared at Freddie. "Her Royal Highness is indisposed and won't be taking tea. A lady-in-waiting will write to you, I'm sure."

There was a flurry of red and gold, and somehow they were all outside the door again, with William Coachman leaning against the carriage door and staring at them with his mouth open.

"They have!" Freddie murmured, staring at the firmly closed door. "They've lost Princess Jane!"

Eight

THEY HAD, BUT IT turned out only temporarily. When Mr. Fountain got home, much later that night, he summoned the children to the drawing room to tell them what had happened. The princess had been found in the palace gardens, blue with cold and most confused. She said that she had been watching the snowflakes while she waited for her dear friend Isabella to arrive.

At this point Isabella made a most unladylike spitting noise.

"Bella!" her father murmured.

"I feel quite sorry for her, if she thinks you are her dear friend," Freddie told Bella coldly.

"You should," Mr. Fountain pointed out. "She really only has her sisters, and none of them are close to her in age. Princess Charlotte is four years younger than her sister. I should think that Princess Jane was sincerely looking forward to Bella's visit."

Everyone looked abashed, even Bella. "I can't help it if she's awfully dull," Bella muttered.

Her father eyed her thoughtfully. "I wonder if she's ever been alone for more than five minutes?" he said.

"Oh, very well!" Bella snapped. "I will go back, and I will pretend to be having a wonderful time."

Mr. Fountain sighed. "You may not be allowed to."

"Why ever not?" Bella asked indignantly. "We weren't very rude. Were we, Rose?"

"You did hit one of the guardsmen, Bella," Rose pointed out.

Mr. Fountain sank back in his chair. "Oh Lord…"

"Papa, they'd just tried to stab Miss Anstruther!" Bella protested.

"Besides, I thought you hated going?" Rose couldn't help laughing as she said it. Bella was like a cat, always on the wrong side of a door. Bella shrugged.

"Why wouldn't we be allowed, sir?" Freddie asked. "I don't think we were that badly behaved. Although the guards officer looked as though he'd like to clap us in irons when he realized he'd let slip the truth about the princess."

"Yes, he was lucky. If it hadn't all been a false alarm, he could have been court-martialed."

"But if she'd disappeared, everyone would have had to know sooner or later, wouldn't they?" Rose asked slowly.

Mr. Fountain looked at her and said nothing. Rose blinked. "They wouldn't!"

"I suppose she is ever so popular," Freddie said slowly.

"It would make everyone very angry if anything happened to her. Sir, what did actually happen? How did she end up in the garden?"

"What do you think?" Mr. Fountain asked. He sounded as though he really wanted to know.

"If she didn't know what happened…" Rose began.

"Perhaps she was drugged?" Freddie asked hopefully. Bella shook her head. "They taste her food. All her cakes have a bite taken out of them first. I'd hate that."

"So…it was magic?" Rose suggested, her voice very quiet, as though it was a dangerous thing to say out loud.

"The nation's little princess was abducted by a spell," Mr. Fountain agreed wearily. "It's all I can think of. And I don't know how it went wrong, either, how she came back. Because surely that wasn't what was meant to happen."

Freddie swallowed. "That's…that's not good, is it, sir… People are going to be…upset."

"They are. Very. I shall have to go back to the palace later—a friendly magical face around at the moment, that's what we need." Mr. Fountain pressed his hands against his eyes for a moment. "Coming straight after that debacle with the Sparrow woman and those poor unfortunate children, this is awful. Disastrous."

"You mean, I can't go back to the palace because of my magic?" Bella said furiously. "That's not fair!"

"Is the princess all right?" Rose had been looking out the window at the snowflakes whirling through the darkness. She wouldn't like to be out in that, and she thought of herself as fairly hardy. Princesses were obviously delicate, and Princess Jane was china fair and slender—or she was on Miss Lockwood's commemorative teapot back at the orphanage, anyway.

"Frozen. They missed her the first time they searched. She was under a bush, half buried in snow, and she had a white lace dress on. It looked like it was woven from snowflakes." Mr. Fountain's mustache shivered. "Poor child. She'll be surrounded even more now." He sighed. "Don't worry, Bella. I will try to arrange for you to go back. The princess asked me if you would while I was making her some rather special cocoa. It just depends...I haven't seen the king yet...He may not want..." He sighed wearily. "I must go back."

"That must be very fine lace to look like snowflakes," Bella murmured, her voice dreamy with longing. She adored clothes. "Was it Talish lace, Papa? The very best cobweb kind? Now that the peace is almost settled, I should think the princess can wear Talish lace again."

Her father stroked her curls, smiling. "Perhaps you will get some for your birthday, little one, but I'm not promising. The princess's dress was Talish, a gift from the peace envoy, but I should think most of the Talish lace coming into the country right now is smuggled."

"Did it really look like snowflakes?" Rose asked. She couldn't imagine how fine it would be. She'd seen Mrs. Jones working on her tatting in the servants' rooms in the evening, but even though it was pretty, you couldn't mistake it for snow.

"Oh, yes," Mr. Fountain assured her. "With little sparkly bits—crystals, I suppose—and the most wonderful pattern. It caught the eye most distractingly." He blinked, remembering it. "I must go, my dears. I will see you in the morning."

* * *

But in the morning, Mr. Fountain was summoned to the palace early by a royal messenger in a livery that cast Bill into a deep depression. Miss Bridges had eyed it with the greatest interest, and then looked him up and down consideringly.

"A week, I'd give it," he muttered to Rose at breakfast. "Less than. You'll see. I'll have a tricorn hat by Sunday, so she can show me off at church." He scraped his bowl mournfully. "I wish I worked in the stables."

"No, you don't," Rose whispered back. She didn't speak out loud belowstairs at the moment, so as not to draw attention to herself. "Jacob's had to sweep from the mews clear out to the street already this morning to get the carriage out. Sarah said so. You know she's sweet on him, and she was worrying about his chilblains." She looked at her bowl sadly. She always got small helpings now, and Isabella never left any breakfast.

Bill shoved his bowl forward, and Mrs. Jones automatically dolloped in another large spoonful of porridge. Bill flicked a glance around the table and swiftly swapped his bowl with Rose's.

She stared at him in amazement. "Thank you! How did you know I wanted—"

"You were staring at that pan like it was your long-lost sister," Bill muttered back. Being from an orphanage too, he was allowed to say that kind of thing without fear of starting a fight. "Shut up and eat."

Rose did as she was told; Bill winked at her and shoved her bowl forward too.

"More? Already?" Mrs. Jones asked. "Well, a growing boy, I suppose…"

Bill nodded, trying to look angelic, which was hard with sticking-out ears and hair that stood up in obstinate spikes however short it was cut. He did have very round and innocent-looking eyes though, which worked to his advantage while he was conducting the great Thursday porridge robbery.

"Stop staring at me," Bill hissed. "They'll suspect." Rose blinked apologetically and started to eat her porridge. Somehow it tasted even more delicious for being filched.

As the breakfast was being cleared, Mrs. Jones pushed a list of errands to be run in front of Rose.

"Shall I go with her? She might fall in a snowdrift," Bill suggested hopefully. The snowfall had been very heavy the previous night.

"I'm sure Rose will manage, Bill," Miss Bridges said, sipping her tea. "Although come to me before you go out, Rose, and I will find you some galoshes."

"Galoshes? She needs a signal flare, not shoes," Bill said under his breath.

"And don't let me forget, Rose, that Mr. Fountain has given me a list for you from Sowerby's, as well."

Rose had no idea what Sowerby's was, but everyone else in the kitchen sucked in their breath, as though it was something that shouldn't be mentioned.

"Magic shop," Bill whispered. "Got a big crocodile in the window. Moves its tail too sometimes. It's a treat. You sure I can't go with her, miss?" he wheedled. "She don't know the way to that place."

"Doesn't," Miss Bridges corrected him absently. "King's English, William. And have you polished the shoes and the silver? I thought not." She eyed him beadily. "You wouldn't be planning a snowball fight with the stableboys, by any chance?"

"No, miss…" Bill said dismally.

The galoshes were made for feet considerably larger than Rose's, and they flapped. Rose slip-slapped her way through the square, dodging snowballs being wildly thrown by a group of little children in the garden. The statues were wearing white fur overcoats, and the grumpy stone bird on the shoulder of one of them had an icicle dripping from its beak. It eyed her as she passed, as though daring her to laugh.

Rose plodded on, trying to remember Miss Bridges's complicated instructions for how to get to Sowerby's. Snow seeped over the tops of the galoshes and through the eyelet holes of her boots. Her toes were going numb already, and Mr. Fountain's old Macintosh boat-cloak crackled in the wind as though it would like to take off. It felt like wearing a smelly tent.

She made it to the grocer's and stood inside the doorway for a moment, enjoying the warmth of the big cast-iron stove. The heat made the delicious smells of the shop even stronger, and Rose shivered her way through the warm pepper- and spice-scented air. The shop was full, as though everyone was lingering on their errands today, not wanting to go back into the snowy wilderness outside. Rose caught the ends of several conversations as she made her way to the counter.

"Poor little thing. Frozen quite solid, they say. Not even a shawl on."

"It isn't natural. Not snow this deep, and not this early in the winter neither!"

"Well, stands to reason it's witchcraft, doesn't it? What else could be doing it? Unless it's a Judgment."

"Let it creep in, then you turn around one day and this is what they're up to!"

"Children crawling into the sewers for shelter. Cruel, it is."

"They had it right in my mother's village, burned the lot of them, they did. That was a long time ago, mind…"

Rose drew her cloak tighter around her and scuttled toward the counter, her mind whirling with frightening images.

As she went out with her purchases, a lady in a jet-trimmed mantle was holding forth to her friend about witchcraft and how it ought to be stopped. Rose wondered if they knew where half the sovereigns in the box behind the counter had come from. Not that she could tell which ones the master had made, but she knew that a lot of the country's gold was magicked. Freddie had told her that without the gold, the country would fall apart. Did no one here know that? Didn't they care?

If they knew what she could do, would these nice-looking people want to stuff her into the glowing stove and burn her?

Rose felt that her heart was a lump of ice, colder than the snow outside.

As the door of the grocer's clanged shut behind her, she looked anxiously up and down the road. It was left from here, she was almost sure, but the high snowdrifts made it hard to get her bearings.

Hordes of small boys were shoveling passageways through the snow, some with shovels that looked suspiciously new. Rose wondered if any hardware stores had been broken into recently. But she gladly scrunched her way along the paths, dodging calls for a penny or even a farthing. The Macintosh cloak protected her when they threw snowballs for not paying.

Sowerby and Son was at the end of a row of shops that Rose had never seen before, a few minutes' trudge from the grocer's. Rose saw the sign swinging from the front and made for it gladly, hoping to warm up again inside. But as she drew closer along the narrow snow path, she saw that the owner and his assistant were outside, with steaming buckets and scrubbing brushes.

"Don't you throw anything!" the assistant told her as she flapped up in her galoshes. "We've heard it all, all right?"

"I wasn't going to," Rose promised. "I've a list." Sowerby's was a small, dark-fronted shop that looked rather like a pharmacy, its windows full of bottles and jars, and little wooden drawers with labels like those in the workroom. The dark glass windows had gilded letters on them, advertising *Esoteric Supplies*, *Exotic Ingredients*, and *Patent Apparatus*, but right now they also had painted slogans in splattery writing: *Witches Beware! Leave Our Children Alone!* And, rather poetically, *Drinkers of Blood Begon* Although Rose wasn't quite convinced about their spelling, which detracted slightly from the message.

The news about Miss Sparrow's strange practices had

clearly spread, she thought, shivering anxiously. And it had gone beyond newspaper articles and grumbling in the grocer's, as far as demonstrations in the street.

"Come in, dear, come in." Mr. Sowerby had a mustache to rival Mr. Fountain's, only his was long rather than wide, trailing in two tails right down beyond his waistcoat buttons. "George, you keep scrubbing. Little monsters. What do you need, dear? Are you new? I don't recognize you."

Rose dropped a curtsy, although she wasn't sure Mr. Sowerby would see it inside her cloak. "I'm Mr. Fountain's new apprentice, sir, and a housemaid. It's irregular. Sir, who painted your windows? They were saying in the grocer that witches made the snow!"

Mr. Sowerby pursed his lips. "Magicians, dear, please, let's not lower ourselves. Arrant nonsense. That snow is real. It would take an unbelievably powerful spell to do something like that." He looked out of the window, frowning, then shook his head. "It couldn't be. Ridiculous idea. I tried to tell the louts who defaced the shop that, but they just threw snowballs at me. And stones," he added grimly. "Luckily the glass is diamond hardened, though that was to stop things getting *out*, not things getting in." He looked at her with bright little eyes. "Fountain's new apprentice. Well. There's a thing."

"Here's the list, sir. Mr. Fountain wants it all urgent, he said." Rose brought out the list, and Mr. Sowerby fetched a set of brass scales onto the counter with a stack of the tiniest weights Rose had ever seen. She supposed magical ingredients must be rather expensive, as she watched Mr. Sowerby weighing the strange dusts and powders into little twists of oiled silk. She had been wondering why a magician would choose to keep a shop, rather than working for the king or doing something else a little more exciting, but as she looked at the towers of jars, she wondered just how much gold it would take to buy all this.

Mr. Sowerby had diamond ear studs, she noticed.

"Your shop is beautiful, sir," she told him shyly, gazing at the shining bottles. The snow had stopped, and sparkling sunlight was streaking through the windows, throwing colored light on the wooden floor.

Mr. Sowerby glanced up at her, as he carefully weighed out an odd licorice-black powder that shimmered and shifted on the scales.

"Father and son, my dear, father and son, for two hundred years. Never a spot of trouble. Until now. You tell your master for me, Solomon Sowerby's compliments, and he'd better get us out of this mess." He shook his head. "Oh, it'll pass. There's been wicked rumors before, I suppose. But never anything like this."

"You couldn't have stopped them?" Rose asked, waving a mittened hand at the windows.

Mr. Sowerby grinned, showing pointed white teeth.

"With my hands tied behind my back, young lady.

But I didn't think that blasting a gang of ruffians to kingdom come would be sensible—not at the moment. Tempting though it was."

"I've done it, Dad. And I've set them to repel anything else. Whitewash or whatever." The boy who'd been cleaning the windows came back into the shop, clanging the buckets.

"Good lad. Have you fed Henry? Did you see Henry, my dear, on your way in?" Mr. Sowerby led Rose over to the window, and she gulped. The odd bench that she'd seen out of the corner of her eye in the far window had a tail, she saw now. And teeth.

"The kitchen boy at home said it was stuffed," Rose murmured, staring at it nervously.

"Oh, so he is, so he is," Mr. Sowerby agreed. "But Henry's not so stuffed he can't manage another meal, tee-hee-hee." He laughed a strange giggling laugh but then stopped abruptly. "Look! George, they're back! Little monsters, not again." He shook his fist at a group of scruffily dressed boys, lugging a can of paint, who were leering at him through the window.

"They won't get it to stick, not this time," George said, folding his arms across his apron grimly. Then he smiled gleefully, his eyes creasing at the corners.

"Henry's hungry, Dad..."

"Ah..." Mr. Sowerby sighed with satisfaction. "You've a point there, George, a very good point."

"He won't eat them, will he?" Rose asked, her voice

squeaking with horror, wondering if she should run out and warn the boys. But then Henry might eat her too!

"He won't get through the window," George said regretfully. "Pity really. But you just watch…"

Rose peered into the window space, seeing now how Henry the crocodile coiled around the display of odd, carved boxes, his scales burnished to a greenish gold, and his teeth like carved ivory. He was stuffed. In fact, Rose could see the stitches where he'd been rather badly sewn up, and there was even a wisp of horsehair poking out between the scales. When Bill had said he moved his head, Rose had thought it must be some sort of clever clockwork. She'd seen a clockwork doll in a toyshop. But there was a feeling about Henry. She couldn't see a key.

The boys outside had been daubing paint on the window for a few minutes now, but it wouldn't stay, and they were getting angry. Presumably because Mr. Sowerby hadn't done anything to them the last time, they weren't afraid of him and George, and now they gave up on the paint and resorted to jeering and catcalls, shouting about witches and child stealers. Rose felt like screaming back at them, saying it was all lies, but she knew it would only make it worse.

The three of them watched in suspenseful silence until the boys began to bang angrily against the window. Then Mr. Sowerby let out a long-held breath and glanced hopefully at George.

"What is it?" Rose asked.

"Watch and see," George muttered back, lifting her onto a tiny embroidered footstool so she had a better view into the window.

Henry's shining scales glinted in the snowy light and flickered as the window shivered. Rose frowned a little. It had twitched. Had it? Was it just the glittering light? No, it had done it again. All at once the window was filled with eight feet of furiously thrashing crocodile, snapping, lunging, and roaring at the terrified boys on the other side of the fragile sheet of glass.

George and Mr. Sowerby howled with laughter as the boys scrambled their way through the snow to escape. Even Rose couldn't help giggling. It was a rather mean thing to do, she supposed—but then the words they'd been painting up were about her. Her laughter died.

Henry slid down the window, his black claws scraping the glass with an eerie shriek, and padded grumpily around the wooden boxes. George pulled out a bucket of something that looked quite disgusting and poured it down in front of him. Rose backed away, shuddering, as Henry went into a slobbering, tearing frenzy in the window. She supposed Bill had never seen Henry at feeding time, or he'd never have said the creature was stuffed.

Rose trailed back home through the snow with the parcels, worrying over what she'd seen. She was almost certain Mr. Sowerby was right, and the fierce winter was nothing to do with magic, despite the strange prickling feeling in her fingers whenever she touched the snow. It was just because it was cold, wasn't it? But that meant nothing if everyone else was equally sure the winter weather was some dreadful spell.

Nine

M R. Fountain hardly seemed to be in the house at all for the next few days. He didn't even go to church on Sunday, which left everyone quite shocked. Bella and Freddie sat alone in the family pew, and Bella was heard to snore quite loudly during the sermon until Freddie poked her. Miss Bridges flinched, but there was nothing she could do.

After the service, magicians were chatting in worried groups, and it was noticeable that several non-magical families had disappeared from the congregation. Rose waved to Mr. Sowerby and George, but Mr. Sowerby's mustache looked limp.

On Monday, the butcher's boy didn't deliver as usual, and Rose and Bill had to go and fetch the meat order. The butcher had a sign in the window, advertising a public meeting on Registration of Dangerous Members of Society. Bill nudged her. "That's you, Rosie." He sniggered.

Rose looked at him miserably. "You don't believe that, do you?"

Bill shrugged uncomfortably. "'Course not. Well, not you, anyway. Reckon Mr. Fountain could be a bit dangerous. But he's on our side, isn't he?"

"There isn't a side!" Rose wailed.

"Oh, I don't know. It's all politics, isn't it? Dull stuff. Jack says there's to be a Frost Fair if this cold snap carries on, first one in thirty years. You want to come with me, on your afternoon off?"

"What's a Frost Fair?" Rose asked, distracted for a moment.

"When the river freezes over," Bill explained. "It hasn't done it for years, not since they rebuilt the bridge. People said it never would again, because the water flows too fast now. But this winter—with the magic an' all—it'll be solid by next week, Jack reckons, and he knows a couple of the boatmen. When it's hard enough to walk on, they build stalls. There's dancing. Maybe even a bear. Will you come, Rose?"

Rose considered. She had never been to a fair— any kind of fair—and the idea of one on the top of a river sounded too charming to miss. "The first in thirty years," she said slowly, not wanting to agree all at once.

"I'll buy you some gingerbread," Bill offered gruffly.

Rose smiled. "Oh, well then…are you sure you want to take a dangerous member of society to a fair?"

Bill scowled. "You're making fun of me. Just say no if you don't want to."

"Oh, I do!" Rose touched his arm just for a second. But he caught her hand and laid it on his sleeve.

"You better hold on. Slippery around here. Knowing you, you'll go arse over backward any minute." But he looked at her mittened hand on his sleeve proudly, and Rose couldn't help smiling.

"I do want to go. But I want you to understand that I'm not dangerous, and neither are Freddie or Bella, or Bella's father. You do believe that, don't you?"

Bill nodded. "'Course," he said airily.

Rose sighed. She had a feeling he'd say anything to keep her hand on his sleeve. She hoped she hadn't done something silly by agreeing to go. She suspected that actually he just wanted to show off by taking a girl to the fair.

Still, it was easier to walk through the snow with Bill to hang on to. He was taller than she was, and he hadn't been burdened with the ridiculous galoshes. But they were both grateful when they reached the square, and they could scuttle down the steps to the kitchen door.

"The meat! At last!" Mrs. Jones threw up her hands. "How'm I ever to get any lunch on? What did you take so long for?"

"There was a sign up in the butcher's," Bill volunteered to try and detract from their lateness. "A meeting. About registering people, like them upstairs." He looked apologetically at Rose, who'd retreated into the corner to take off her cloak and galoshes.

Mrs. Jones looked to Miss Bridges, as though she wasn't sure what to say. Rose was sure she wanted to approve but thought she'd better not.

Susan wasn't as circumspect. "Good. At least someone's got the sense to see where all our troubles have come from!" She stared at Rose, her lip curling as though the other girl was beyond contempt.

"And just what is that meant to mean?" Miss Bridges returned, striking quick as a snake, before Rose could reply. Not that she'd meant to, anyway.

Susan backed away a step, and folded her arms. Her voice shook a little, but Rose couldn't tell if that was anger or fear at her own daring in standing up to the housekeeper, who could easily dismiss her without a second thought. "The princess. She got stolen by a magician, that's what everyone says. And there was that other one, that the master was mixed up with. That *she* was mixed up with." Susan nodded to Rose. "Trying to drink children's blood. The police aren't doing anything, are they? The Runners? No one's stopping them," she added sulkily.

"Stopping whom?" Miss Bridges asked contemptuously. "Are you implying that because of one renegade—the accusation you've made about the princess is just too ridiculous even to dismiss—all magicians should be outlawed?"

Susan nodded. "They're all murderers," she muttered, but she sounded doubtful, as though she thought she might have gone too far.

"So will you be going to this meeting?" Miss Bridges inquired, her tone one of mild interest.

"Don't know when it is." Susan eyed Miss Bridges resentfully. "I'll be working anyway, won't I?"

"You will?" Miss Bridges raised her eyebrows slightly. "You wish to work for a murderer? I had assumed this was a rather long-winded way of giving your notice."

Susan gasped, just for a second. Then she took a deep breath and nodded. "Very well then. I'm giving it. There."

Miss Bridges had seated herself at the table and was now pouring a delicate cupful of tea. She stirred it slowly then sipped, looking at Susan over the gilded rim of the cup. "How will you obtain another position without references?" she asked thoughtfully, as though it was something that had just this moment struck her.

Rose, Bill, Sarah and Mrs. Jones all swiveled their eyes to Susan.

She blinked. "Without references..." she said quietly.

"Mmm." Miss Bridges added a smidgen more sugar to her tea with a delicate pair of sugar tongs. Then she looked up at Susan, smiling slightly.

Susan took a step toward the table, one hand lifted pleadingly. Then she dropped her eyes to the tabletop and murmured, "I'll need to be mending Miss Isabella's best lace that evening, miss. She tore it, Sunday."

Miss Bridges nodded regally and frowned at a stray

leaf in her tea. "Do come to me for some silk thread, Susan," was all she said.

* * *

Everyone crept about their duties for the rest of the morning, aware that a line had been drawn, that loyalty mattered now, however uncomfortable they found it. Miss Bridges sent Rose to clean the study. She stared at Rose so coldly as Rose drew breath to ask why Susan was not to clean it, as the study was always Susan's job, that Rose simply shut her mouth with a snap and went to fetch some finer dusters.

She had been in the study before, but only once, to be looked over by Mr. Fountain, when she first came to the house. She had been too overawed to notice much about the room, except its owner, and that the rug needed a proper clean.

Now she drew in a slow breath of delight as she closed the door quietly behind her. The room even smelled good—of strange spices, lifted with a tinge of exciting power, the power that wafted freely from the instruments hanging on the walls and standing on the shelves.

She laid her dusters gently on a chair and spun around slowly. It was as though she could see the magic behind her eyes—much more than in the workroom on the floor above. It floated and sparkled around the strange machines, colors softly changing, too fast and yet too slow for her to catch quite when it happened.

A great deal of the magic seemed to lead in trails over to the large wing chair by the window, Rose realized at last. Her heart jumped into her mouth as she saw a hand draped across the arm. The master was still at the palace, wasn't he? Miss Bridges had said nothing about him being in the study—in fact, she'd told Rose to take the opportunity to bring the Oriental rug down for beating if she had time.

Unsure whether to expect a burglar—though why would a burglar sit down?—Rose crept forward to find Mr. Fountain fast asleep in the chair, frowning even in his sleep, a newspaper draped across his knees.

How on earth had he got back without anyone knowing? Miss Bridges would be most upset, Rose was sure. Mr. Fountain had unconventional manners and occasionally opened his own front door with a latchkey, which was low and quite inappropriate. Rose thought that secretly Miss Bridges would like to be in charge of a much larger household—the attics where she and Susan and Sarah slept were enormous, with lots more rooms beyond theirs. Clearly the Fountain house could fit in a great many more servants if they were wanted, and there wasn't a shortage of money. How could there be, when the master could just magic some more up? Although Rose suspected he probably wasn't supposed to do that. Perhaps Mr. Fountain just had no taste for ceremony. It would be nice to have a butler though. A butler would add a little something extra, Rose felt.

Rose looked at him uncertainly. His mustache was a little askew. Mr. Fountain had a mirror in every room of the house, so that he could make sure his mustache was in perfect points, all the time, and he slept with it in a net. Somehow, the sight of half the jet-black whiskers pushed out of line by the side of the chair was terribly upsetting. Mr. Fountain looked almost human, instead of the demigod Rose and all the household were used to thinking of him as.

Rose tiptoed away, feeling as if she were being rude by staring at him. She looked dubiously around the room, wondering where to start. All the apparatus was dusty. She knew that Mr. Fountain's desk was bespelled to sting anyone who touched it—she had tried—and she wondered if the strange contraptions around the walls were the same. Susan must have hated cleaning this room. She despised magic so, and she couldn't have ignored it here. Charitably, Rose wondered if that was why she had done it so badly, but she admitted after a few seconds that Susan didn't really need an excuse.

Although Susan had never mentioned the machines or even the stinging desk, perhaps she had just been told not to touch it because of important papers. Would she even have been able to see the magic at all?

Rose reached out gingerly with a duster, hoping not

to be turned immediately to stone. But nothing happened. The intricate, clock-like mechanism in front of her just got rather shinier. Then it clicked. Rose stepped back anxiously, hoping that she hadn't broken it. The hundreds of little brass wheels turned and meshed, and then glitched again. Rose peered at it worriedly, wondering what the machine *did*. Was it merely measuring something, or was something being made here? There was a little slot at the bottom, as though something was meant to come out.

The wheels and gears were still dusty. Rose sighed gently, hoping she was doing the right thing, and a soft cloud of glittering dust rose up out of the clockwork. She wafted it away with her duster, and the wheels spun and chimed again.

"Goodness, Rose, that hasn't worked in years!"

Rose nearly fell into the machine, but Mr. Fountain caught her just before the spinning wheel sliced her fingers off.

"I'm not surprised," she snapped, fright making her brave. "It hadn't had a proper clean in I don't know how long. All those fancy bits were bunged up with dust."

Mr. Fountain nodded. "You're probably right. The other maid hates it in here. She leaves such an unpleasant stench of fear that I put very strong Don't Notice Me spells on most of the room—it's no bigger than a broom cupboard for her now."

"Wouldn't it have been easier just to ask for someone else to clean it?" Rose asked, genuinely puzzled.

"Probably…" Mr. Fountain blinked thoughtfully, as though this was an interesting idea. "But I never remembered to do that at the right time. Dust in the works though. I hadn't thought of that."

Rose sighed very quietly. "I don't think I'll be able to get it all set to rights today, sir."

"No, no, much appreciated, Rose." Mr. Fountain looked around the room, as though seeing it properly for the first time. "I do see what you mean," he agreed apologetically. "I'm sorry, Rose. I'm not at my best today."

"We thought you were still at the palace, sir," Rose ventured. "Would you like me to go and tell Miss Bridges you're back? I'm sure she'd send up some tea."

"Hah! Tea!" Mr. Fountain snorted with laughter. "It'll take more than that, Rose. Look at this." He thrust the newspaper at her, his expression grim.

Rose took it and read the front page, puzzling out the small type. "Oh! There's to be a meeting about this too, sir. There was a sign up, in the butcher's."

"The butcher's?"

Rose wondered for a second if Mr. Fountain knew what a butcher's was. "Yes, sir. The butcher's boy didn't deliver this morning. I went to the shop to fetch the order. Miss Bridges wrote a note."

"I should imagine she did." Mr. Fountain smiled slightly. "I shouldn't think the butcher's boy will be the only one, Rose, not after this." He twitched the newspaper out of her hands and read the headline again.

PARLIAMENT DEMANDS REGISTRATION FOR MAGIC USERS

"Short-sighted bunch of idiots," he muttered. "If it is all a spell, who do they think is going to get them out of it? If they've put us all in jail, they'll be fighting it on their own."

Rose gasped. "Jail?"

Mr. Fountain looked up quickly and patted her arm.

"It won't come to that, Rose, I promise you."

"What did you mean, sir, about it being a spell? The winter? Or Princess Jane?" Rose twisted her hands in her apron worriedly.

"Both. They may perhaps be connected. There's something I can't quite lay my finger on." Mr. Fountain rubbed a hand across his face. "Or then again, maybe neither. I can hardly concentrate on what's going on, what with running around trying to stop the Honorable Member for Tibbleswick from persuading His Majesty to have me beheaded." Mr. Fountain looked at Rose, eyeing her wearily. "If it is a spell, this ridiculous weather, it's a damned good one. I can't find a chink in it, Rose. Not the merest crack."

Rose stared back, her heart thudding painfully. Mr. Fountain was an incredibly powerful magician.

He and two colleagues (unfortunately deceased) had discovered the secret of making gold, and he had entered into a very profitable arrangement with the government about how exactly his discovery should be used. Rose had known him to be overcome by a glamour, but to hear him say so clearly that he couldn't unravel this mystery was terrifying. He had to be able to. He could do anything, couldn't he?

"You will, sir," she promised him, watching the frown lines smooth slightly. She looked around the room. "Can't any of these help? What does this one do?" The brass wheels were still turning and clicking beside them.

Mr. Fountain laughed again, and this time he sounded as though he really thought it was funny, almost in spite of himself. "Oh, Rose. It counts dust. Grains of dust. That's all."

* * *

There was something nasty put through the letterbox the next morning. Everyone in the square knew a magician lived at number 23; it was no secret. Rose, having been made to clear it up, was starting to feel much less sympathetic toward the frightened people gossiping and whispering in the streets. She wondered how long it would be before someone decided to fight back and what would happen then.

Bill met her as she put the brushes and cleaning cloths back, and waved away her moans about the mess. "It's on! The Frost Fair. The ice is holding and they're building stalls. The pantry boy from across the square told me while I was out sweeping a path to the front steps."

"Sweeping a path to the steps so people could put horse—horse *dung*—through the letterbox!" Rose snapped. She was handicapped by the insistence on manners at St. Bridget's. One did not say those words.

"Come on, Rose," Bill pleaded. "You said you'd go. You're not weaseling out of it, are you?"

"No." Rose sighed. "I'll go. I'm just—scared. Things keep getting worse. The master was at the palace at the crack of dawn again today. Freddie and I haven't had a proper lesson for ages."

"Don't tell Mr. Freddie about tomorrow afternoon!" Bill warned. "I'm not traipsing round a fair with *him*. I'd look a right idiot."

Despite her fears, and the increasingly hysterical newspaper headlines, Rose couldn't help looking forward to the afternoon out. She had told Bill that she didn't want to leave the house together—Susan already teased him about being sweet on her, and Rose didn't want to make it worse. Even Miss Bridges had given her an odd look that morning, and she had always been Rose's great champion. Bill didn't seem to care that hardly anyone belowstairs spoke to Rose apart from him, but she wasn't going to rub his nose in it.

They met at the corner of the square, Rose bundled up in her Macintosh cloak again. She'd almost left off the hated galoshes but had added them at the last minute. She did not want to get her feet any wetter than she had to, as it was well-known that wet feet led to all sorts of horrible illnesses and now was not the time to contract a putrid sore throat. She had put on her good bonnet to try and take away the effect of the ugly galoshes.

Rose eyed Bill a little worriedly, hoping that he wasn't going to start anything silly. She knew that going to the Frost Fair with him would make anyone else think they were sweethearts, but Bill had better not try kissing her.

Luckily Bill seemed more concerned with looking at the lowering snow clouds than Rose. "Can't believe it. Look, there's going to be another fall tonight, I'll bet. It ain't natural, Rose. I swear, not in October." He looked down at her in surprise when she said nothing. "Hey! Has the master said something to you? Is it a spell, all this?"

Rose looked around nervously, not that she really expected anyone would be spying on a couple of servant kids. Still, it would be disastrous if anyone heard them. Then she eyed Bill. She was pretty sure she could trust him—even though he was as silly about magic as the rest of the servants, he'd still seemed to be on her side. Did he think she was capable of turning him to stone or feeding him to a dragon? He was remarkably rude to her if he did, but Rose would rather have it that way.

"He thinks so," she muttered. "You mustn't say anything! To anyone, do you promise?" *I should have made him promise first*, she thought wildly, watching the color drain out of his face, leaving it the same color as the grubby snow around their feet.

"Yeah, I promise," Bill whispered. He looked sick.

"You said it was magic first!" Rose protested. "I was only telling you that you were right!"

"I know, but…if he says so…" Bill wiped a hand over his face, which was covered in a sheen of sweat, despite the freezing air. "Well, then it really is, isn't it?" He grinned shamefacedly. "I was just moaning, you know, about the weather, like Mrs. Jones does all the time, with her rheumatics telling her there's rain on the way. I didn't really mean it…" He sighed. "Maybe I did. No one's ever known a Frost Fair in October. What's he going to do about it, then?"

"He doesn't know who's making it," Rose admitted.

"But he'll find out! And then he'll get them," she added loyally, though Mr. Fountain had not been in a very martial spirit the last time she'd seen him.

Bill nodded, looking more cheerful. "'Course he will. He's a genius, ain't he? Don't you worry, Rose. He can do anything."

Rose wished she could believe him. But she looked

around at the London streets covered in a foot of snow, with battlements of icicles dripping from all the roofs; the scale of the magic was so huge that she couldn't see how one man could fight against it. Perhaps Mr. Fountain was recruiting other magicians to help. He must be—unless he was worried about creating a panic, she supposed. She couldn't help wondering if he'd told the king. If the snow and the attack on the princess were linked together somehow—and the snow was still falling—well, she wasn't sure what that meant…

"We're nearly there, Rose. I can hear music!" Bill forgot the snow spell in an instant, content to leave magic to those who understood it.

The scraping of a violin brought even Rose out of her worried daze, and they both hurried forward, making for the river.

"We'll go down the Fothergill steps," Bill told her excitedly.

The steps down to the river had been swept clear of snow but were still slippery, and Bill handed her down graciously. The sight of the huge river, set solid between the bridges, was so amazing that Rose forgot to worry about what had caused the scene. Instead, she was swept up in the excitement. Everyone on the river was there either to enjoy themselves or to make money, preferably both. All along the central channel of the river, a double line of booths had been set up, selling food, large amounts of drink, and every kind of entertainment.

"Tuppence to enter!" A large man shouldered himself in front of them, wearing an odd uniform of a bright red jacket, most old-fashioned, and all wound around with mufflers.

"I've only got tuppence," Rose whispered sadly to Bill. She was still paying back the cost of her dresses, and Miss Bridges only allowed her a few pennies at a time.

"Oh, just let 'em in, Ezra, poor little things." An equally large woman, made even larger by the huge quantity of shawls she wore, lurched toward them, carrying a black bottle which Rose strongly suspected was full of spirits. Still, she wasn't going to complain. The waterman let them pass, with much grumbling about losing his trade, and Rose and Bill hurried into the fair, stammering their thanks.

"What'll we do first?" Bill asked eagerly. "You'll never guess, Rose: Barney from next door told me this morning there's an elephant!"

"Don't elephants come from Africa and India?" Rose asked doubtfully, as she skidded along on the pitted ice. "The poor thing won't like it out here, not at all."

But Bill was right. Up at the end of the lane of stalls was a large enclosure of rickety fencing with an enormous and morose-looking elephant. Rose had known in theory what an elephant looked like from the large number of books about foreign missionaries in the orphanage schoolroom, but the tiny illustrations—even those with elephants carrying Indian princes in little houses on their backs—had not prepared her for the reality. The beast's legs were wider than she was, even in a Macintosh cloak, she thought, staring open-mouthed.

The elephant was harnessed to a sort of sled, fancifully decorated like a ship, and the owner was charging a shilling a ride. There were a surprising number of customers.

Bill looked at the elephant regretfully. "I'd rather ride on its back. Not much point in being dragged around after it. All you'd see's that strange little tail."

"And a whole shilling!" Rose pointed out.

"Yeah, I haven't got one of those, either." Bill grinned. "Good, though, eh?"

Rose nodded. "It's wonderful." She gazed around at the stalls. "Do you think there's anything I can buy for tuppence? I wish I had more."

Bill chewed his lip thoughtfully. "We can look," he suggested, but he sounded somewhat doubtful. "Anyway, I'll buy you something. I said I'd buy you gingerbread, didn't I?"

Rose shook her head. "You shouldn't," she told him, smiling. "But I'd like something I can keep. This might never happen again. You said it wasn't meant to happen at all." She shook off the memory of how wrong it all was, determined to enjoy it while she could. It wasn't as if there was anything she could do, after all. Rose was used to being insignificant. Orphans were never special.

The uneasy thought floated at the back of her mind that insignificant was sometimes easier too.

"What about this?" Bill suggested, as they started back down the line of stalls. "Look, it's got the elephant on it." Rose peered into the booth, where a strange machine had been set up, almost as magical-looking as those in Mr. Fountain's study. A boy a little older than Bill was stroking ink on to a block of metal letters and fixing them into the machine.

"Brand new picture of the Frost Fair," he droned, as though he was sick of saying it. "With the elephant added. Poetry extra. Your name printed on for tuppence."

"You can put my name on it?" Rose asked, fascinated. She had never seen a printing press, and she had no idea how they worked, even such an old-fashioned one as this.

"'Course I can," the boy muttered, rolling his eyes. "You want it or not?"

"Yes." Rose nodded frantically. The elephant was rather odd-looking, with a hump like a camel and an over-long trunk trailing round its feet, but it was still clearly an elephant. She wanted it on her wall. "My name's Rose."

The boy searched through his tray of letters. "No surname?"

Rose shook her head, flushing. "Just Rose, please."

"If you say so. There." He pulled down a wooden handle and peeled a piece of paper off the block. "Mind, the ink's still wet."

Rose gazed at it delightedly. TO COMMEMORATE A REMARKABLY SEVERE FROST. PRINTED ON THE RIVER, OCTOBER 1843, and then her name, in ornate lettering, and the elephant below. It was wonderful, and she handed over her two pence gladly. She wafted the handbill to and fro to dry the ink before folding it carefully into her reticule.

"Don't you want one?" she asked Bill.

"I'd rather have gingerbread. Come on." And Bill set off again, dragging her along, sniffing out a sweet-meat stall.

They walked along the rest of the stalls, munching happily. The gingerbread was shaped into snowflakes, and gilded. The luxury of eating gold! It seemed almost sinful. And it tasted wonderful, the rich, peppery spices warming them from inside.

"We should get back." Bill sighed.

Rose nodded. "There's one last stall over there though," she pleaded. "We could look at that quickly and then go?" She didn't want to go back to the house and the magic, and her fear. Not just yet.

The last stall was on its own and had a white canvas roof decorated with silver ribbons. A crowd of people was in front of it, jostling to see.

"It's probably another of those 'find the lady' games," Bill suggested, as they tried to peer round the edges.

Rose shook her head. There had been lots of those, fleecing customers out of their money, and she knew Bill had been tempted—luckily, gingerbread had tempted him more. This was different. There was a smell about it, like Mr. Fountain's study. Her heart thudded unpleasantly—was someone performing magic on the ice? A magic stall?

Bill was wriggling and pushing his way through the crowd, and Rose was more frightened of losing him than she was of whatever was in the white tent. She followed, making judicious use of her elbows and trying to look innocent.

"Look at that!" Bill whispered.

Rose just nodded, unable to stop staring. The stall was full of little glass globes, each containing a miniature scene, tiny houses, or streets. The one closest to Rose and Bill showed the river and the bridge.

Rose had seen snow globes before—Bella had one in her room, with a little girl in it, feeding doves. But Bella's globe was still, until you shook it to make the snow fall—which Rose had never dared to do.

These ones moved. The figures danced, and the water running under the bridge rippled. It wasn't clockwork. When the stallholder shook a globe for a beautifully dressed lady who looked as though she might actually buy one, the little figures all rushed to hold on to something. Rose shook her head, unbelieving. They were the prettiest things she'd ever seen. She couldn't imagine how much they'd cost, and when the stallholder told the lady only a guinea, she looked at Bill, her mouth falling open. They knew how much magic cost. These delicate baubles were worth a hundred times more than that.

Rose looked at the globes distrustfully. It couldn't be right. The stallholder was a young man, with curiously light eyes, a strange icy blue. Rose wondered if he was the magician who'd created the globes or just an assistant. He had a slightly strange voice, an accent she didn't recognize.

The lady who wanted a snow globe was arguing with her husband now. He was shaking his head and muttering. Surely he couldn't think it was too expensive? Didn't he realize what a bargain he was getting?

His voice rose, and Rose could hear him properly.

"I won't have it in the house! You know that magic's dangerous. Look at the weather! Too much of the stuff floating around. Put it back."

The lady sighed, stroking the snow globe lovingly with one finger as she handed it back to the stallholder. He tried to reason with the husband, but the man wouldn't listen and started to walk away, turning back and shouting, "You should be ashamed, showing these abominations off here! We've had enough after what you *magicians* did to our princess!"

A surge of whispering and muttering ran through the crowd, as though they'd been entranced by the globes, and had now just realized what they were. There was a strange hissing noise, and Rose realized, shivering, that it was a crowd of people all saying the same words, over and over again. *The Princess…the Princess…*

Everyone believes it was magic, she thought to herself. *And they're blaming all the magicians.*

The first globe hit the canvas at the back of the stall and didn't break, though Rose swore she could hear a high, thin scream as it hurtled through the air. Then Bill grabbed her, diving sideways as the crowd surged forward and tipped the trestle table over, sending a jeweled rush of sparkling glass onto the ice. Huddled against the side of the tent, Rose and Bill watched the stallholder crying, pleading, begging them not to do it—or was he begging the globes not to shatter? He was scooping as many of them as he could rescue into his apron, cradling them and cooing in a rush of unrecognizable words.

They were so beautiful. Even if she didn't trust them, Rose couldn't bear the globes to break amongst all those stamping feet. She tucked the nearest one under her skirt, feeling it pulsing against her ankle, painfully cold even through her stocking. It wasn't glass. Even lying on ice, glass couldn't be so cold that it burned. Curled still against the canvas, Rose thought warm thoughts as hard as she could. She felt as though the snow globe were turning her to ice, so she would shatter too.

"Ah!" The stallholder made a desperate dart forward, but he was too late. The burly waterman, Ezra, who'd tried to charge Rose and Bill for entry, had lifted his heavy oilskin boot. The snow globe splintered with an eerie shriek, and the ice-eyed man wailed as he searched the crystal pieces. They didn't cut him—in fact, Rose realized, shivering, they were melting back into the ice, as though they were a strange kind of ice themselves. Their owner scrabbled up the little figures, thrusting them squeaking into a pocket, and the waterman spat.

"There. We'll do that for all your magic. Your kind aren't welcome here anymore. Go on, get out of it." And he kicked the pole holding up the white canopy, sending the canvas slewing down across the ice and into the stallholder. It didn't knock him down. He stood watching the waterman walk away, the ice from the shattered globe dripping between his fingers. His eyes were darker now and colder, and the air around seemed suddenly to prickle with cold as he stared after the striding man. The humble, pleading posture was forgotten.

Rose wasn't sure how long the waterman would last. The crowd straggled away, tittering. No one else seemed to have felt the sharp thrill of magic. Bill hauled Rose up, eyeing the stallholder cautiously, and Rose picked up the snow globe, shivering as it seemed to send a piercing, icy cold running through her veins.

"Sir…"

The ice-eyed man stared at her, sharp-eyed.

He hadn't noticed them before, Rose realized. She wished they'd stayed still. Hesitantly, she held out the snow globe, her hands trembling as it stung them with cold. "It rolled… I hid it…"

"Oh." The man smiled slowly, and his voice softened to a purr. "You are a good girl. I thank you."

"Come on, Rose," Bill muttered, tugging her arm.

"Your companion does not trust me, but you—you have some knowledge, hmm?" The smile was fixed now, and Rose and Bill edged out of the collapsing stall as fast as they could. The man followed, step by step, his eyes stabbing Rose. Then he seemed to change his mind, shook his head. "No. Servant children. I am wrong, of course. Just a good little girl." The man smiled wider, showing very small, very white teeth, little tiny pearls. "Keep it, dear heart. A present."

Rose nodded and turned and ran.

"Who was he?" Bill gasped, as they reached the top of the Fothergill stairs again and stopped for breath.

Rose shrugged. "I don't know. A magician though, definitely." Rose wished she had met more magicians—with only Mr. Fountain and Alethea Sparrow to compare the stallholder to, it was hard to pin down why the man had scared her so. Perhaps she was wrong about him. He had been kind to her after all. But she still didn't trust him.

"That thing's worth a fortune," Bill whispered, staring at the snow globe still clutched in Rose's mittened hands. "Why'd he give it you?"

"Don't know that either." Rose looked at it, the little scene glittering against the wool. It had stopped burning her now, and it looked innocent, like a pretty toy. But Rose was sure it wasn't. There had to be something more to it—and to the man who'd given it to her. She wished she'd had the courage to refuse the gift, but at the time it hadn't felt like a choice. Staring down at the delicate bauble, Rose wondered how many others the ice-eyed man had given away.

Skaters on a frozen pond, whirling and skimming among the snowflakes. Bill had put his finger on the most important thing. The stallholder had to have some reason for giving Rose the globe—and for selling them at only a guinea apiece to start with. There was definitely something wrong there.

"Hide it away, for heaven's sake," Bill pleaded. "Someone'll steal it otherwise, and anyway, I don't like it."

Rose looked up in surprise. She didn't either, but she couldn't say quite why. She hadn't expected Bill to pick up on the strange sensation the globe gave off—she'd thought he would call it a silly trinket, that was all.

Even if it had cost Rose a hundred guineas, she still wouldn't have trusted it. She tucked it reluctantly into her little bag, wishing she could just stuff it into a snowdrift instead. But she had a feeling that wouldn't work. It might follow her.

It seemed to weigh her down as they walked back, though it wasn't really that heavy. Rose dragged her feet, still cursed with those stupid galoshes, and sighed.

"What's the matter? He really scared you, di'n't he?" Bill asked.

"He could see I had magic. He thought he'd made a mistake when he saw our clothes properly, but actually he was right." She sighed miserably. "I don't know what I am either. A housemaid or—or something else. Something everyone hates."

"I don't," Bill said quickly.

Rose smiled at him briefly. "No. I'm glad about that. I'd miss you if you didn't talk to me. But seeing the way everybody hissed at him, Bill…even if I don't trust that man, he was what I am. I do know, really, you see. I knew then, when everyone was hating him. Me. Us."

Bill nodded. "That's why you're glooming then?" His voice was doubtful. "Isn't it good to know what you are?"

Rose looked at him, shocked. He'd surprised her again. "Well, yes. I suppose that's right. I should be happy. Proud, even." She nodded firmly. "You're right. I should stop creeping around and just tell everyone."

Rose looked thoughtfully at the passersby, and Bill grabbed her arm.

"Bearing in mind how things are, maybe not right now, eh?"

Ten

Rose was looking forward to asking Freddie and Mr. Fountain about the snow globe at her next lesson. She wondered if Mr. Fountain knew its strange creator—she had decided that the ice-eyed man must have made the globes because he had loved them so much. But although Freddie was fascinated by the toy and sat gazing into the wild snow for ages, Rose never had a chance to show it to Mr. Fountain.

"He's late again," Freddie murmured, gently shaking the snow globe and giggling as the skaters shook their tiny fists at him.

"I don't mind." Rose didn't even look up from *Prendergast*, the magical primer that she and Freddie were supposed to memorize. She was trying to find out about weather magic, but the book was surprisingly cagey. Weather magic was apparently "dangerous, difficult, and inadvisable." Which was not a whole lot of use. "I'd much rather read this than wash the windows."

"What's the point of washing windows?" Freddie asked. "They only get dirty again. Waste of effort if you ask me. Really, I think servants are quite unnecessary. Your job is just busy-work."

Rose only sighed and ignored him. There was no point rising. Freddie would complain soon enough if the servants stopped running around after him.

Freddie sniggered complacently, and Rose yawned. She had built up the fire, and it was pleasantly warm in the workroom, despite the weather. She glanced out of the window to see if it was snowing again. Not yet, but the sky was leaden gray and heavy looking. There would be another fall soon. She gazed dreamily out at the black trees across the square—and then jumped. A face had inserted itself between her and the trees, shimmering in the glass.

"Freddie…" Rose whispered.

"What?"

"Mr. Fountain's here…"

Freddie sat up suddenly and looked at the door in horror, then turned to glare at Rose. "No, he isn't! Don't do that sort of thing to me, Rose. It isn't fair. Oh." At this point, he finally noticed his master floating in the window glass. "Good afternoon, sir."

"And to you, Frederick, now that you've finally deigned to notice that I'm here. Rose, you need to daydream more often. I've been waiting for you to stare at something shiny for over an hour."

"I'm doing this?" Rose asked, looking worried. She couldn't feel that she was. She had never made anything that could see her back before.

"Yes and no. I'm using your ability to do it, let's say. Listen, I don't have long. As you may have worked out"—here, the image eyed Freddie critically—"I am still at the palace. I'm so sorry to miss your lesson yet again, but I have no choice. Things are—difficult."

"Are you all right?" Rose asked him shyly, and Mr. Fountain gave her a weary smile.

"Thank you, Rose. I'm perfectly fine. I haven't slept, that's all. I have been trying to obtain an audience with the king. He is understandably somewhat reluctant."

"But you see him every day!" Freddie burst out.

"Not since he realized that a magician—or possibly a conspiracy of magicians—tried to kidnap his daughter," Mr. Fountain replied shortly.

"Oh." Freddie seemed remarkably cowed by this news, Rose thought. She looked at him worriedly. He had been very matter-of-fact about his friends and relatives at the palace, but she had a feeling he would be deeply upset if any of that changed.

"As far as I can see, the only way to get back into the royal family's good graces is to find out what happened to Princess Jane—and catch who did it if I possibly can." Being split into bits by windowpanes didn't help, but Mr. Fountain looked particularly downhearted. Rose and Freddie exchanged anxious glances. "I shall be moving into my rooms at the palace. I must be there, to search and to counteract any more stupid rumors. The place is buzzing like an evil beehive." The window image looked up at them both, strangely distorted by the snowflakes that were starting to fall behind it. "I'm so sorry—your lessons, and you've already missed so many this last week. We will have time soon, I promise, but this has to come first."

"Of course it does, sir." Freddie got up, and went over to the window. He reached out tentatively to touch the glass, a more affectionate gesture than Rose had ever seen him use to his master in the flesh. "If you can't solve this, who knows what will happen. But, sir, can't we help? We can't just sit here and read *Prendergast's Perfect Primer*. We'll go mad wondering what's happening."

"Oh, yes!" Rose agreed, jumping up and coming closer to the window. She could feel the way Mr. Fountain was borrowing her magic now, a strange tickling feeling in her fingers and somewhere deep in the back of her head.

"We could do something, couldn't we?" Freddie pleaded.

"If you're moving to the palace all the time, you'll need all your things. We could bring those, just to start with," Rose suggested. The idea of Mr. Fountain existing without his mustache nets and brushes, and his cologne, was unthinkable.

Freddie wrinkled his nose. Rose thought he'd probably imagined himself doing something more dramatic than being a delivery boy, but she nudged him and glowered, and he nodded obediently.

"Yes…yes, I suppose that would be useful. If you could speak to Miss Bridges about packing my personal effects, Rose. And you, Freddie, make a list of the things I shall want from the workroom and my study. Well, go on, boy, find a pencil!"

Freddie turned his back on the window to make an anguished face at Rose, but she slipped out of the door to find Miss Bridges, smiling sweetly at him.

* * *

There wasn't a great deal of room left in the carriage for Freddie and Rose. Once Mr. Fountain's piles of smart, gold-monogrammed leather luggage had been inserted and packed around with bags and boxes of books, instruments and ingredients, Rose wondered if it might be easier just to sit on the box with the coachman. She was left clutching a large parcel of rather sharp-smelling powder, which was slowly leaking out of the corner of the wrapping, and an astrolabe, just in case it might be useful.

The snow was still falling, and the drive to the palace in the gathering dusk seemed to take forever as the coachman peered ahead through the murk.

Mr. Fountain had made sure there was a page to

meet them at the door this time, and Rose pretended to ignore the amused glances of the soldiers as she and Freddie trailed in, dragging all their luggage. She made sure the parcel leaked powder over the nearest one's black shiny boots and reminded herself to keep an eye on him, to see if it did anything interesting.

The pageboy looked disgusted at having to carry a carpetbag full of squashy parcels and set off too fast for them to keep up with him along the scarlet carpets. Rose was torn between horror at getting lost—what if she blundered into the king?—and the impossibility of walking quickly when at every turn there was something fascinating to look at.

"Oh, do come on, Rose!" Freddie muttered crossly, over his armful of books. Luckily, he knew where he was going, or at least he said he did. Rose didn't know. Everywhere was gilded and sparkly and carpeted. They could, just possibly, have been walking around and around the same corridor the entire time.

What was odd, Rose thought, was that such a wonderfully grand place could also feel so flat. After one got over it being a palace, and the fact that everything looked so expensive and beautiful, it was strangely cold. Almost sterile.

Rose hugged the leaking parcel tightly as they processed along yet another corridor, lined with dark oil paintings and gas lamps in ornate, fussy golden sconces. The page boy had relented and come back, muttering about slow coaches and people who had their worldly goods tied up with string. Freddie was ignoring him in a lordly fashion while clearly dying to answer back, and Rose was just ignoring him.

She worked it out just as they walked past an amazing white and gilt room, with a golden ceiling that seemed to be melting and dripping down the walls.

There was no magic.

She had only been at the Fountain house for a few weeks, but the building was so steeped in magic that every painting, every floorboard even, abovestairs at least, simply vibrated with inner life. Here, there was nothing. It was an empty prettiness, devoid of character, and it felt sadly disappointing. She supposed she had imagined it like some fairy-tale castle, and it did look like it. But there was nothing fairy-like underneath the gilt, only stone.

The page boy stopped suddenly and flung open a door. Rose cannoned into Freddie, and the pungent parcel went into its final collapse at last. Rose felt it was a great pity that it covered Freddie and not the obnoxious page boy. He made a very fast escape, and Freddie and Rose were left at the door of Mr. Fountain's rooms.

"Good Lord." Mr. Fountain hurried over in his shirtsleeves, looking somewhat horrified. "Freddie, what on earth have you done to yourself?"

"It wasn't me!" Freddie protested. "Rose dropped it. Why does everyone always blame me?"

"What is it?" Rose asked, feeling a little worried. There was an awful lot of it, all over Freddie, and if it was poisonous...

Mr. Fountain picked up a pinch of it gingerly, between finger and thumb, and sniffed it. "Experimental guano."

"It isn't!" Freddie glared at Rose. "Of all the things to drop on me, Rose. Bird droppings. I shall never forgive you." He shuddered, brushing the loathsome powder from his jacket.

Rose joined in, brushing his sleeves. "I didn't mean to. You know I didn't. Why on earth do you have that much bird—bird leavings?" She added the last bit in a discreet whisper.

Mr. Fountain seemed to be trying not to laugh. "I just thought it might come in useful. Strong source of ammonia, very powerful chemical. I've no idea why you brought it, Freddie. It wasn't on the list."

Freddie flushed slightly, his pale skin firing up, and Rose thought shrewdly that he had probably gotten bored with the list from the workroom and just started stuffing things into bags.

"Go in there and brush yourself down." Mr. Fountain shooed him toward a door. "I'll send for someone to bring the rest of the bags."

Rose had imagined Mr. Fountain's room at the palace as just that, one room, and probably rather small. Actually, it was more like a series of enormous apartments, leading out of each other, and arranged as a study, drawing room, and bedroom. Everything was decorated in a Chinese style, and there seemed to be dragons everywhere.

"The late king was very fond of Eastern decoration," Mr. Fountain explained, seeing Rose staring at a chair that had been tortured into the shape of a water lily.

"Don't sit in it. It's spiky." He smiled. "I brought a great many cushions from home."

Judging from his rooms, the Counselor to the Royal Mint was an honored member of the royal household—or had been, at any rate.

Freddie came out of the dressing room looking rather better, but he still smelled odd, and his smooth, yellow hair was sticking up—something that even being imprisoned in a cellar by a mad witch hadn't reduced him to. He looked completely miserable, and Rose felt quite guilty, even though she still felt it was largely his own fault.

"Aloysius." A quiet voice spoke from the doorway. Rose turned to see a slender, bearded man standing there, watching them with piercing green eyes. She took a nervous step backward, and Freddie scuttled out of her way, as if he thought she might douse him in guano again.

Mr. Fountain bowed, and now that he was safely out of Rose's way, Freddie did too. Rose hastily curtsied as low as she could without falling over. She didn't know the correct etiquette for meeting the king, but she was sure curtsying came into it.

King Albert walked further into the room and sat

down in the water-lily chair. An expression of acute discomfort passed fleetingly over his face and was replaced with a polite mask. Royalty, obviously, did not comment on the furnishings.

"You wished to see me, Aloysius Fountain," the king continued quietly.

Rose watched Mr. Fountain lick his lips. She had never seen him nervous before. "Your Majesty. I am deeply grateful that you have condescended…"

The king waved a hand irritably. "Spare me, Aloysius. Tell me the truth. I have always felt I could trust you until now. I am here against the advice of all my counselors. Tell me that you were not involved with these scoundrels who kidnapped dearest Jane."

Mr. Fountain stared back at him, eye to eye. "If I had kidnapped the princess, sire, you would not have found her under a bush in the garden. She would not have been found at all."

The king glared at him for a moment, and Rose trembled, wondering if she was about to see her employer arrested for treason. But then the king laughed shortly. "You're right. I have never known you to make a mistake, Aloysius. They were magicians, weren't they? The rumors are true?"

"I fear so, Your Majesty," Mr. Fountain agreed. "There are so few traces. I am trying…I am in the process of moving into my apartments here, so as to investigate more easily."

"Good." The king eyed Freddie and Rose expectantly, and Rose stared sideways at Freddie, wondering what she was supposed to do.

"My apprentices, Frederick and Rose."

The king sat up and winced as a sharp petal drove into some portion of his anatomy. "*She* is a magician?" he asked interestedly. There was a slight edge of disbelief.

Rose stared sadly at the floor. She had hoped that in her lovely new clothes she didn't look quite so much like a guttersnipe orphan, but it didn't seem to have worked.

"Indeed, sire. Very talented, despite an unorthodox upbringing." Mr. Fountain beckoned to Rose. "And Frederick is George Paxton's boy, you may remember? Related to one of your equerries, Raphael Cressy."

"Another of them?" The king looked doubtfully at Freddie and shifted the water-lily chair back a little.

"A *distant* relative," Mr. Fountain added reassuringly. Freddie tried hard not to appear dim but only succeeded in looking manic, making Rose desperate to giggle. She made a strange snorting noise and flushed scarlet. She sounded like a pig in front of the king!

The king ignored her. "Aloysius, have you found anything? Anything at all? Jane still has no idea what happened. She says she was watching the snow falling from her window, and the next thing she remembers is that she was out in it."

138

Mr. Fountain sighed. "Sire, I'm sorry. I can feel no traces of magic in the princess's sitting room, none at all. And yet it must have been a spell. I don't see how it can have been anything else. The garden, where she was found, there are hints there, frozen somehow into the snow…But how she was taken from one to the other, I simply don't know."

"So all my guards, all our precautions, are they any use?" The king was clutching the arms of the uncomfortable chair tightly, his eyes fixed on Mr. Fountain's face.

The magician gazed back uncomfortably. "I fear not, sire," he admitted, his voice very quiet. "A close personal guard, perhaps—but even then, they could be defeated by a well-executed glamour…"

King Albert sighed. Then he seemed to square his shoulders, and he inspected Rose and Freddie closely.

"Are these the children who defeated that awful woman? The ones you told me about?"

"Yes, sire." Mr. Fountain's face was watchful, and his voice was cautious. A prickly feeling ran up Rose's spine. Something was going on here, something that her master was not quite happy about. She glanced at Freddie, but his face was politely blank. His fingernails were driven into his fists though, as if he was trying to keep himself under control.

"Surely the best guard for my daughter would be one who could fight back against these kidnappers, assassins, whatever they are, using similar methods…" the king mused. "And one who could remain undetected. A secret guard. Perhaps a child, a girl…"

"Sire, are you really asking—" Mr. Fountain's voice was its usual purr, but a hint of anger was vibrating through it.

"Yes, Aloysius, I am. This is *my daughter*."

"Rose is someone else's daughter!" Mr. Fountain snapped. "My apprentice, my ward!"

"I'm no one's daughter, sir," Rose broke in quietly. "At least, no one who wanted me."

"You don't know that," Mr. Fountain told her. "I'm responsible for you, Rose. I can't let you do this."

"I'll do it!" Freddie gasped.

The king smiled, and for a second, Rose saw that there *was* a sort of magic in the palace, a powerful bond between this man and his subjects. Even she, as a destitute child, someone who had never come closer to the sovereign than seeing a coronation mug, had looked on the royal family with awe. Now, like Freddie, she would do anything for the king. Even if it meant risking her own life, which Mr. Fountain obviously thought it did.

The king beckoned to Freddie and the boy approached him, looking more humble than Rose had ever seen him. The king seemed to grow taller as Freddie came nearer. "I know you would, Frederick, and I am grateful. I will remember your offer. But the girl is more useful—at the moment. I'm sorry."

Freddie's face fell, and he sent Rose a hurt, resentful glance. Rose blinked back apologetically. She didn't *want* to endanger her own life exactly; it just seemed to have happened, and obviously one had to if one was asked…She would be quite happy to let Freddie do it if he wanted.

"Will you be my daughter's guard, Rose?" the king asked her. "I will tell her you are a new maid. Even she won't know what you really are. It's her birthday very soon—I shall explain to my wife that now Jane will be eight, she needs another servant-companion of her own age."

Rose blinked. She didn't know exactly how old she was, but she certainly wasn't seven. Closer to ten or eleven, she thought. But perhaps even a girl three years older was more of a companion than a lady-in-waiting.

"She is my apprentice!" Mr. Fountain protested faintly. "I need her! For research!"

"How is dear Isabella?" the king inquired. "She is of an age with Jane. Such a pity that her talents have not yet begun to show. She would have been even more ideal…"

"Indeed, a *very* great pity that so far she has not manifested even the merest smidgen of magic," Mr. Fountain agreed quickly, sounding as though he thought it was completely the opposite.

The king gazed at him thoughtfully, and Fountain sighed. "Oh, very well. But I shall require Rose to report to me daily, and I shall be most displeased if anything happens to her!"

The king's voice was somber as he replied. "My dear Aloysius. If anything happens to her, it will be because it has also happened to my daughter. And if that should occur, the mood of the populace being what it is, I would not give one farthing for the continued safety of any magician or sorcerer or magician's apprentice in the city. Your apprentice is guarding your life, as well as that of the princess."

Mr. Fountain sank into a chair, clearly forgetting that it was infernally rude to do this without being invited to sit in the presence of the king. Freddie made a tiny move forward, as though to stop him, but then thought better of it.

"Why can we not see what is going on? How is it being made, this strange, unseasonal winter? Is it connected to the disappearance of the princess? I feel it must be, but I am at my wits' end, sire!" He ran his fingers into his perfectly combed hair, wrenching at the oiled curls, which showed he really was upset. He sighed deeply. "Very well, sire. I shall allow you to borrow Rose, though it goes against my better nature to leave a child in such a situation. Freddie, I shall need you here to help me in my researches. For the moment, you will need to go back to the house, have someone pack Rose's things and your own, and return at once. My household is at your service, sire," he murmured ruefully.

King Albert nodded. Clearly, Rose realized, he had never had any doubt that it would be.

Eleven

T HE KING WAS NOT used to waiting for things. He stood up and ushered Rose to the door with a wave of one hand heavily weighted with rings.

"Wait!" Mr. Fountain strode after them, inserting himself between Rose and the king, one velvet sleeve barring Rose from the door. "Not yet. A few hours, sire. That's all I ask. She is a very capable child but only a child. She has never been instructed in the defensive use of her magic. Rose's magic is powerful, but undirected power could do more harm than good." Breathing fast, he stared into the king's eyes for a second before he dropped his gaze to become the perfect courtier again. "She will be a stronger guard for the little princess if she has some idea what she is doing," he said gently.

The king stared at him, at the upstart magician who had defied his orders, and sighed. "You're right, Aloysius, I suppose." He sat down, carefully choosing a less exotic chair this time. "I will watch."

Mr. Fountain's eyebrows snapped up, and Rose

gazed at the king in horror, but they could hardly say no.

"Carry on." The king steepled his fingers together and leaned back in the chair, looking very much like someone expecting a good show.

Freddie sat down on a small stool next to him. He was carefully not smirking, but Rose could see he felt like it. She supposed it was only fair—she had stolen his coveted assignment after all.

"I'm not sure quite how much Your Majesty will appreciate…" Mr. Fountain murmured, but the king stared at him frostily and he sighed. "Very well. Rose. I understand that His Majesty wishes you to be in the nature of a spy, an undercover agent. You know a little about being a lady's maid from looking after Isabella, I suppose?"

Rose gave him a doubtful look. "I don't know if I could do what a princess would need, sir," she murmured, imagining complicated rules about which crown Princess Jane should wear for breakfast on rainy Thursdays.

The king waved this away dismissively. "There are ladies-in-waiting. I shouldn't think there will be much for you to do."

Rose gave Mr. Fountain a panicked look. She didn't like not having anything to do. It felt wrong.

"Dusting, Rose," her master told her firmly. "There's always dusting. And listening. Remember that spell I taught you for hearing lies?"

Rose nodded, gabbling in her relief—something she knew she could do. "Oh, yes, sir. When you stroke a feather through the air to show you the truth, and I could use a feather from the duster!"

"Good girl. You see. And protection spells. What have we studied that you could use for protection, now...?" He twirled his mustache thoughtfully.

"She could hit them with the duster..." Freddie muttered, and everyone glared at him. "You know she can't do anything useful!" he protested.

"I can!" Rose snapped. "Just as useful as you could, anyway!"

Freddie flushed angrily. "I've been studying for y-years..." he stammered.

Rose caught the king's frown and remembered suddenly that she and Freddie and Mr. Fountain were all in danger here. Protecting the princess wasn't just about scoring points off Freddie. If anything happened to her, it was quite clear, all the magicians in the country would be held responsible, whether it was fair or not.

Rose turned around, the skirt of her good wool frock swinging. She was thinking as fast as she could, pulling together all her strange talents for creating pictures, and as she swung back to face them all, she cast out one hand and threw what appeared to be a fiery demon at Freddie and the king. It flared around them, roaring.

"Good God!" Mr. Fountain struggled out of his coat

and used it to douse the creature. "How on earth did you do that? And please, Rose, think! We are supposed to be protecting the princess, which means we do not want to immolate her father. Or Freddie, I suppose."

"It wasn't real," Rose assured him. "I just borrowed the reflection of the fire on that strange screen with the tigers. I thought it might scare somebody who was attacking the princess." She looked apologetically at the king. "I just wanted you to see I can do things," she explained.

The king stood up, shaking out his lacy cuffs, as though he thought they might be singed. "Quite. Most impressive. Well. I have a meeting with Lord Venn, the Talish envoy. I will be back...in a while. Hm. Good." He walked to the door in a very stately manner that almost concealed the slight tremor around his knees.

Freddie uncurled himself from around the back of his stool and scowled. "It wouldn't stop a magician. They'd know at once it was only illusion. I knew, of course."

Rose smiled at him. He would swear blind he wasn't scared, but she'd seen his face. And she was willing to bet that a fire monster would upset anyone, even the most trained magician, if it popped up when they weren't expecting it. It would throw them off balance for a few seconds, and that was enough for Rose to call for help.

Besides, fire melted snow.

* * *

Mr. Fountain had been working at a gentle pace in their previous lessons. "I was trying to give you some sense of the myriad intricacies of the universe," he mourned, pacing up and down the lily-patterned carpet after King Albert made his hurried exit. "Get you to appreciate the beauty and wonder of your heritage." He turned around and stabbed a finger at Rose. "And instead it all comes down to this, showing you how to throw things."

"I think she needs to know rather more than that, sir," Freddie pointed out. He was still eyeing Rose rather cautiously since she'd set the fire-beast on him.

"No." Mr. Fountain shook his head gloomily. "It's all about throwing things. Bullets. Arrows. Fire monsters. No imagination. No creativity."

"Girls can't throw for anything," Freddie declared loftily. He spoiled the effect rather by giving Rose a nervous look as he said it.

"I liked the fire monster," Rose said in a small voice. She had been quite proud of it.

"Oh, Rose. It was a wonderful spell." Mr. Fountain smiled at her, but it was clearly an effort. "But I wanted you to be making things like that for the fun of it, not to frighten people. Don't you see?"

Rose nodded. "It is for the safety of the British Empire, sir," she reminded him timidly.

That finally made Mr. Fountain laugh. "They should put you on a handbill, dear Rose. Come, we don't have much time." He removed his frock coat, revealing a smart purple velvet waistcoat, rolled up his sleeves, and smoothed his mustache to business-like points. Then he shot suddenly sideways, making Rose squeal, and darted a hand down a very small hole in the wainscoting. He came back up holding a very surprised-looking rat.

"Ugh." For once, Rose and Freddie were in agreement.

"Don't be silly," Mr. Fountain murmured absently, waving a hand at the rat, which shivered, squeaked miserably, and turned into a small, toothy man in a hairy brown suit.

Rose gasped. This sort of thing only happened in fairy stories.

"It's just a glamour," Freddie said doubtfully, trying not to sound too impressed.

"Of course it isn't," his master snapped. "I'm doing it, not him. It's an extremely complicated enchantment, so I'd thank you to stop chattering and concentrate. Right. Rose. This rat—because he's still a rat inside, you know—is about to learn that you have stolen the cache of bacon rind he had concealed in a hole under the palace's third meat larder. He is not going to be very happy about this."

"I didn't!" Rose protested. "Oh! I see what you mean. But what am I supposed to do? Oh no..." She backed away a few paces as the rat man turned and stared at her, showing his horribly yellowish teeth. He had ceased to look pitiful, and now she noticed his glittery little eyes, his claw-like fingernails, and the scuttling speed with which he moved—toward her.

He's a rat. Only a rat, Rose tried to tell herself. But she couldn't stop thinking about the rats in the orphanage dormitories, who nibbled the girls' toes if they left them sticking out. This rat wanted more than toes.

Traps. Cheese. Poison. Things one did to rats whirled through Rose's head. She didn't have any of them.

Freddie was grinning at her, blast him. Oh well. Mr. Fountain had said himself that it was really only about throwing things at people. Rose grabbed the spiky water-lily chair and hit the rat with it, quite hard. The poor thing sagged in the middle and disappeared, and suddenly there was a standard-sized brown rat in Mr. Fountain's hand again, looking even more confused than before. The magician kindly released it back into the hole in the wainscoting before he turned to look thoughtfully at Rose.

Rose blushed and stared at her toes.

"Well…I have to admit I'd expected a magical solution, but it did work. A chair in the stomach certainly distracted him from the bacon rind." Mr. Fountain folded his arms. "I think perhaps you need a more balanced opponent. A bespelled rodent isn't really an adequate sparring partner."

Freddie was looking around the walls, as though he was expecting Mr. Fountain to seize a spider. Then he glanced back at Rose and his master and worked out what was going on.

"Oh no…that isn't fair! I can't hit her, sir! She's a girl!"

Mr. Fountain sighed. "Frederick, you are an evil magician. You do not care that Rose is a girl. You are trying to assassinate a princess, who is also, surprisingly enough, a girl. Use some imagination, boy!"

They kept at it for two more exhausting hours, spell after spell, until it really did start to feel as though it was all about throwing things. Rose was as white as milk, and Freddie looked as though the next bolt of blue lightning would have him in a puddle on the floor.

"Good. Good," Mr. Fountain muttered approvingly as Rose pinned Freddie to the wall with a backhanded flick of his own spell. "Ah. Rose, straighten your hair. His Majesty is coming."

Rose rather liked royalty looking at her sideways. It made her feel slightly better about her mission, that she was obviously a little bit frightening. She still didn't feel very frightening. Rose felt as though the spells were all in a jumbled pile in the back of her mind. The chances of rummaging through the mess and grabbing the right one just when she needed it seemed slim.

"I will arrange for you to report back daily," Mr. Fountain told her firmly. Rose hugged Freddie—she was almost as surprised as he was—and scuttled after the king as he strode off down the corridor.

She realized as they walked that he must have abandoned his entourage to visit her master. A number of worried-looking courtiers who'd been lurking on corners gradually formed a little procession behind them. None of them looked particularly happy to see Rose, and she wondered if they knew what she was there to do—perhaps not, as the king had wanted it to be so secret. Probably they had just assumed that she was Fountain's servant and mistrusted her as they did him. How had the disgraced magician worked his way back into the king's favor? And what was his spy doing following His Majesty toward the princesses' suite? Rose could feel the questions vibrating in the air.

They were heading toward the royal family's private quarters now. The atmosphere of the rooms was changing, the grand red and gold corridors with their warlike portraits of kings on horseback and bloody battle scenes had given way to papered walls in a softer pattern, without quite so much ornamental gilding and gore. The king seemed to have changed too. He didn't look back to check that Rose was following—he knew she would be, Rose supposed, since he had ordered her to—but she could see his face as he turned the corners. He was smiling now, and he was walking faster. Rose sighed a silent breath. He loved the children, then. It wasn't just that Jane and Charlotte were the nation's darlings, and they were making him the most loved monarch in centuries.

Of course, that meant he would probably risk anything to save them.

Including Rose.

* * *

As they neared the door to the princesses' rooms, a page boy sprang into action and flung it open, bowing in the same movement so that Rose only saw the top of his head as King Albert swept by. The door led into an anteroom, where there was another page boy— possibly the first one's twin, Rose wondered, as the tops of their heads looked exactly the same. The boy threw open another door, revealing a beautiful drawing room, with pink-and-white-striped wallpaper and the largest dollhouse Rose had ever seen almost covering one wall. Admittedly, Rose had only ever seen one other dollhouse, the one in Bella's schoolroom, but this one was a mansion by comparison.

"Papa! It isn't Wednesday. What are you doing here?" A girl a little younger than Rose jumped up and ran to the king, smiling delightedly. It looked as though she was going to throw her arms around his waist, but at the last minute she pulled back and curtsied low to the ground. The king raised her up and held her in his arms, but Rose couldn't watch. Did she only see him on Wednesdays? And she had to curtsy to her own father? No wonder Bella didn't like coming to tea.

"Darling Jane, I've brought you a present." The king waved an arm at Rose, and Rose blinked indignantly. Really! He might as well have tied a bow around her! One did not give people as presents.

"This is Rose, your new maid. It is very nearly your birthday after all."

The young princess gazed at Rose in surprise. Everyone else in the room looked equally shocked, and those the king couldn't see glared at Rose. She peered at them under her eyelashes as she curtsied to the princess and shrugged inside. It would be just like home.

"It's very kind of you, Papa, but I have so many maids…" Princess Jane said doubtfully.

Her father waved her objections away. "This girl is your own age, Jane dear. She will be good company for you. Keep her with you always, won't you? Promise me?"

Jane nodded, but she glanced in confusion at Rose, clearly wondering why this was so important. Then she smiled at her father, more worried about keeping him with her than his strange gift. "Perhaps I should add her to the pile?" she suggested innocently, turning to show him a table laden with presents. "I just can't wait another three days!" she complained, laughing. "They're so tempting. And Charlotte has already got as far as undoing the ribbons on two of them; we had to hide them at the back!"

"Sire..." One of the courtiers who had followed Rose and the king coughed meaningfully. "Your meeting with Lord Venn—you excused yourself for only a few minutes..."

The king sighed and stroked his daughter's hair.

"I have to go now, dearest. Rose will entertain you, I'm sure." He glanced at Rose as he turned away, his smile fading and a dark, agonized look settling in his eyes. He nodded slightly, and Rose nodded back. She didn't know what she was agreeing to—except that she would do what she could. She wondered what else he was expecting.

The page boy closed the door behind him, and the whole room seemed to sigh and relax, as though everyone in it had been windup dolls, and their clockwork had run down now that their owner had gone to play with something else.

The princess smiled graciously at Rose. "I'm afraid I'm not sure what your duties are to be," she confessed. "Papa doesn't usually order my staff. But it was very sweet of him to give you to me." She appeared to have no idea how strange this sounded, and Rose didn't dare point it out.

"I'll do whatever you ask, Your Highness," she promised, bobbing a curtsy.

Princess Jane looked at her thoughtfully. "Most people say that, but I believe you will," she murmured. Then she shook her head slightly, staring at Rose wide-eyed, as though there was something worrying yet rather interesting about her.

* * *

Mr. Fountain had laid protective wards all around the princesses' rooms—after the first attack. No one had thought to ask him to do it before, as there hadn't been any need. Now it meant that these rooms felt far friendlier to Rose than anywhere else in the palace, with their warm tingle of protective magic. But despite the welcoming spells, her new life was unbelievably strange. There was absolutely nothing for her to do.

Princess Jane and Princess Charlotte had ladies-in-waiting, waiting around to do everything. They had their own cook, who came to the suite every morning to take orders, and always looked depressed as Princess Jane really did prefer bread and butter to cake and fancy dishes as Bella had said, and Princess Charlotte was far too little for the kind of rich food he'd like to cook. The most exciting things he was allowed to make were gingerbread men for Princess Charlotte, and he made the most of it. They were the most beautiful gingerbread men that Rose could imagine, with intricately iced outfits and spun-sugar hair.

There were also three governesses, a dancing master, a gaggle of page boys, and several equerries, including Freddie's cousin Raphael, but he was in disgrace and just moped around looking even dimmer than he usually did—or so Freddie claimed in the one snatched moment he and Rose had in the corridor when Mr. Fountain and the princess just happened to be going in the same direction. The palace's usual maids did all the cleaning and tidying, and somehow managed to be almost invisible and completely silent. They wouldn't give Rose lessons in that, even when she did manage to catch them.

So Rose was reduced to lurking behind Princess Jane and trying to look useful. She would have found it infuriating, but of course the princess was used to having people around her all the time. Rose had borrowed—stolen, actually—a feather duster from one of the maidservants, and she flicked it around when anyone seemed to be looking at her suspiciously. So far, everyone seemed to accept that she was just a rather strange present from the king. They all resented her being there, but no one realized she was actually a magical bodyguard. At least, she hoped no one did. If they did work it out, someone might start fighting her, and she didn't want to unleash the fiery monsters or any of her other tricks until she really had to.

Even though Mr. Fountain and Freddie were at the palace too, it was impossible to see them for more than a moment, as she'd promised to stay with the princess all the time. She'd even slept the two nights she'd been there on a little folding bed just outside the princess's bedroom. It wasn't comfortable, and she hadn't slept well—she kept having the strangest dreams, which was very unusual for her. She had woken twice the first night with only a sense of unease, but last night had been much worse. There had been pale-faced figures with black hoods pacing through her dreams, and they had seemed *real*. One of them had been behind Princess Jane's drawing room curtains, grinning. Rose had been forced to get out of bed and creep into the drawing room, where she had picked up the poker from the fireplace, trying to remember the incantations Freddie had taught her for different metals. She repeated the words a little doubtfully, staring at the lump of metal in her hand. An iron poker seemed so unmagical. If it didn't work, she supposed she could just rely on the old-fashioned method and hit someone with it. But as she reached the end of the spell, the cold metal seemed to grow warm and soft in her hand, as though she could reshape it into whatever she needed. Rose gripped it tightly, feeling it quiver, and made herself draw the curtains sharply apart.

There was nothing there. Nothing except an indrawn breath—a feeling of waiting—and a pattern of ice crystals sprayed across the windowpane, like a bunch of tasteful flowers.

But they *had* been there—whoever *they* were. Rose was almost sure, yet not quite sure enough to sound the alarm. She crept back to bed, still clutching the poker.

Curled up in her blankets, she reached under her pillow for the snow globe. She still didn't like it very much, but it was company of a sort. In a palace full of suspicious, magic-hating courtiers, such a wonderfully magical object made her feel less alone and less of a pariah. She had taken to slipping it in her pocket, and the biting cold had dulled to a refreshing chill that was quite pleasant in the overheated palace.

One of the skaters looked very like Bill, just with better hair. She missed Bill. Rose yawned and wondered if he missed her too.

* * *

Rose sat up, peering through the open door. Daylight, almost. No hooded figures had stolen the princess in the night.

Princess Jane was still asleep, so she could sit and think for a moment. Rose blinked and realized that the fire in the princess's room was burning already—one of the maids must have been in to light it, and she hadn't noticed. Rose wasn't sure if she felt more guilty as a fellow servant or as a hopeless bodyguard. Maybe she and Freddie should take shifts through the night, so someone was always watching? But then, it would probably be a national scandal if a boy slept outside Princess Jane's bedroom. And it would make it obvious that something was going on—she was undercover, that was the point. Rose sighed. It was chilly in the corridor, and the young princess was still fast asleep. Pulling the blanket off her bed, she wrapped it around herself and padded into the room, settling in front of the fire. She put the poker back on its hook and stared into the flames. Should she tell Mr. Fountain about her odd dreams? They seemed rather silly and insubstantial in the grayish morning light. She couldn't set the whole palace searching and fretting because of frost flowers.

Seven o'clock chimed on the pretty clock on the marble mantelpiece. It was carved from dark wood and had flowers and birds all over. It wasn't the kind of thing that Rose had expected to see in a princess's bedroom though—she'd thought there'd be rather more gold.

"It's made out of a bit of a ship."

Rose tried to stand up, still wrapped in her blanket, and pitched forward, banging her head on the fireplace and just escaping falling into the fire. Dizzy, with odd white flashes behind her eyes, she barely felt the little hands hauling her up and leading her to the bed. She came back to herself spluttering as the princess tried to hold a glass of water to her lips. Horrified, she tried to jump up again.

"Stop it! You'll fall over, and you're already going to have a most disfiguring bruise."

"I'm sorry, Your Highness..." Rose whispered.

"Oh, don't worry. I shouldn't think anyone will notice. I don't have to meet anyone today. Otherwise, you probably would have to cover it up. It wouldn't do if you looked as though someone had attacked you, would it? People might not think you were much good at protecting me—or too good, maybe?" The princess glanced thoughtfully at Rose before clamping a wet face cloth to her forehead. "You had better not let Papa see it. He'll think someone tried to kidnap me again, and the fussing has only just died down."

"You know?" Rose blinked at her. She felt stupid, but she wasn't sure how much of that was due to the blow to the head.

"Of course!" Princess Jane glared at her. "Oh, it took me the rest of the day to work it out, but you sleep in front of my door! And, I'm sorry, but if Papa really wanted to give me a maid, it would be a trained lady's maid or a dresser. You are quite ordinary."

That's what you think. Rose suppressed a smile, but the princess's next words froze her.

"So ordinary that I can't quite work out what Papa is doing. There must be something rather special about you, something that just isn't obvious. I had thought that you might be trained in hand-to-hand combat, one of those amazing Eastern sorts, ju-jitsu or karate. But I don't think you'd fall into the fireplace if you were. So I'm not quite sure what it is. You seem ordinary, but there's something I can't quite pin down." She smiled at Rose. "You thought I was stupid, didn't you? Lady Alice said that you came from Mr. Fountain's household, so I suppose you've heard about me from Isabella, and she finds me terribly boring. I can't help liking bread and butter, you know. Cake is nice sometimes, but I find I really can't be excited about it." Rose swallowed. Princess Jane was much more frightening on her own, when not surrounded by a horde of ladies-in-waiting.

The princess was still watching her thoughtfully. Rose couldn't think straight herself. It was too terrifying to be sitting on a princess's bed, next to a princess. A princess who was helpfully holding a cold cloth on her head and tutting about the possibility of a black eye. She seemed to think it was not at all the thing for one's maids to appear battered.

Rose's dizzy mind returned to the clock. "It's made out of a ship?"

Princess Jane nodded. "Yes. Most of my furniture is, you know. Sailors like to carve things, apparently, and they will keep sending me it all. It would be awfully bad manners to send any of it away. It's partly why I have the doll's house." She waved a graceful hand at the enormous white and gold confection, just visible in her drawing room. "Papa asked the navy to mention discreetly to the hands that miniature furniture would be more useful at the moment. But the doll's house has had to be enlarged twice already."

"Sailors made your bed as well?" Rose asked, putting out a hand to stroke the carved woodwork.

"Almost. It was a present from His Majesty's dock-yards. It's a lateen-rigged caravel." Princess Jane's tone of voice suggested that she had learned this off by heart, quite possibly at the same time as rather a lot of other nautical terms. "The figurehead is supposed to look like me, but I don't think it does, do you?"

Rose peered diplomatically around at the foot of the bed, which was shaped like a tiny ship, albeit with pink silk curtains falling from a rather eccentrically placed mast instead of sails. She had already noticed the fig-urehead, and she thought it really bore a remarkable resemblance to Jane. It wasn't just the pretty, regular features, and the neatly banded hair; it was something to do with the rather wooden expression.

But she shook her head firmly, even though she regretted it a second later. "No. Ow. I mean, I'm sorry, Your Highness."

"You definitely aren't trained in unarmed combat," Princess Jane murmured. "A display came to the palace to entertain us a few weeks ago. All adepts of the fight-ing arts are very brave and long-suffering. You would be able to climb a mountain with a broken leg, and you certainly wouldn't be saying *ow* for a mere black eye." Rose tried to look blank and possibly a little faint, but the princess didn't seem very convinced. "You didn't answer the question properly."

"No, Your Highness. It doesn't look like you. Your coloring is much more natural."

"Well, of course it is. Mine isn't painted!" Princess Jane sighed with just a touch of irritation. "Are you feeling better? We've a little time before anyone else comes." She hopped up and fetched a satin dressing gown. Rose scrambled to help her into it, but she shrugged it on anyhow, batting Rose's hands away. "Oh, don't fuss, I can do it myself. Come on. Charlotte is too little to play with the dollhouse properly, and it's much better with someone else."

Rose obediently followed her into the drawing room and kneeled in front of the house. It was perfect, painted white to look like stuccoed stone, and crusted with balconies, pediments, and columns. A tiny gilded frieze ran around the building just below the roof, illustrating the exciting events of the sea battle that had established Jane as the darling princess of the nation, with a group of heathen gods and goddesses of the sea watching in the main pediment while riding a number of interesting sea creatures. Several of the goddesses had tails and were coiling them about rather indiscreetly.

"Help me undo this." Jane pointed to the front of the house, and Rose leaned close to see what she was trying to do. She smiled delightedly when she realized that the sea goddess's trident was actually a little hook that held the front of the house together, and when Jane slipped it, the whole front hinged out to reveal the rooms inside.

"I can't touch that, Your Highness!" Rose gasped.

It was too delicate, too pretty, too precious. Without meaning to, she folded her hands behind her back.

"You are supposed to do whatever I tell you," Princess Jane pointed out, her eyes flashing, the wooden expression leaving her face for the first time. She looked much better that way, Rose noted at the back of her mind, and wished that the princess melted more often. She hadn't realized before, but the frozen look was so sad.

"I don't know how," Rose whispered apologetically.

"Look." The princess handed her a tiny doll that might have been Rose herself in a pretty cotton, print gown. "A housemaid. And here are her brushes. You can't get that wrong, can you? Sweep the nursery, please."

By the time a shocked lady-in-waiting discovered them, Rose had progressed to being the cook, not without a pang at the thought of Mrs. Jones back at her house. The doll's kitchen even had tiny versions of Mrs. Jones's adored copper jelly molds and a rather more impressive patent stove.

The princess squashed all doubts about the suitability of playing with Rose and the dollhouse by reminding everyone that Rose was supposed to be a companion, the king had said so, which no one could deny. She told Rose in front of at least six ladies-in-waiting and the dancing master that she was to have care of the dollhouse as her special duty. "Charlotte is always messing it up," she added to Rose in a hissing whisper. "And I can't abide it being untidy."

In fact, Rose thought that little Princess Charlotte was a most unnaturally neat four-year-old, but she would never dare tell Princess Jane that. Charlotte adored the dollhouse, partly because it was really her sister's, and once she realized that Rose was there to help her play with it, she spent the whole afternoon—while Jane was with her governesses in the school-room next door—making Rose enact grand parties in the ballroom.

The parties almost always ended with the house catching fire and all the dolls having to be lowered off the balconies in lace handkerchiefs borrowed from the ladies-in-waiting. The ladies were doubtful about this at first but soon discovered that Charlotte was much less inclined to interrupt good gossiping time if she was allowed to play with Rose. Lady Alice even smiled at Rose when Princess Jane finished her lessons and came to fetch her.

Jane looked accusingly at the dolls all fainting on the carpet, and Rose started to tidy them away quickly when one of the pages announced a visitor.

Visitors to the princesses' rooms were quite rare, even more so since the kidnap attempt, Rose gathered, so Jane and Charlotte were distracted at once, and even Rose looked round eagerly.

When she saw who it was, she had to stop herself from running to greet him, which just showed how much she was missing the Fountain house, as she'd never normally want to run to Freddie.

He bowed exquisitely and winked at Rose when the princesses couldn't see.

"Have you brought a message from Mr. Fountain, Frederick?" Princess Jane inquired.

"Yes, Your Highness. My master sent me to ask if I could be of service in entertaining you, as you asked a week or so ago. I was due to come with Miss Isabella if you remember."

Princess Jane clapped her hands delightedly. "Oh, yes! Are you going to do tricks?"

Rose looked at Freddie worriedly. His magic could be rather hit and miss, and she thought this sounded somewhat risky.

"May I borrow your maid, Your Highness? To assist me?" Freddie beckoned anxiously to Rose, and she hurried over as soon as Jane had nodded graciously. The princesses and the ladies-in-waiting settled themselves in a semicircle around Freddie to watch.

"Are you sure you can do this?" Rose muttered worriedly, as she helped Freddie spread a cloth over a little table.

"He isn't doing most of it. I am," a purring voice told her from somewhere around Freddie's waistcoat.

"Gus!" Rose whispered in delight. She really had missed the cat. There were no pets in the palace apart from the queen's very spoiled little Pekingese lapdog.

"Don't give him away!" Freddie hissed.

"I couldn't if I wanted to. I don't know where he is!" Rose snapped back.

"Watch chain," Freddie muttered out of the corner of his mouth, and Rose realized that he had a very smart gold watch chain draped across the front of his waistcoat with little golden charms hanging from it. She had supposed he had just dressed up for the princesses, but now she saw that one of the charms was a tiny golden cat, with one sapphire eye and one topaz. It winked at her, the sapphire blinking out of sight for the merest instant.

"Ohhh," Rose murmured in relief, and Freddie shot her an irritated glance.

"I'm not that bad!"

"It took me a while to develop the transformation spell," Gus whispered. "I thought I might come and help you. Perhaps. The house is horribly quiet without you all, and I'm sick of sleeping. Scaring the servants is entertaining for a day or two, but Susan screaming just makes my ears hurt now."

Rose gave a grateful little sigh. She was sure Gus would decide to stay. He hated to miss interesting magic, and the chance to catch a royal kidnapper would appeal to his predatory nature.

"Hurry up, Frederick," Gus murmured. "Don't keep the audience waiting, as any good performer knows."

In truth, they were rather good conjurors, Freddie maintaining a courtly patter and Gus providing most of the power for the pretty little tricks. There was a worrying moment when Freddie made Princess Charlotte's bracelet disappear and couldn't get it back again, but at last it reappeared with an audible pop, floating above her head, and everyone applauded. Freddie, who had gone greenish-white with horror, growled at his watch chain.

They ended by giving magical flowers that glittered and sang, though a little out of tune, to both princesses, and Freddie requested Rose's help to pack up again. Under cover of the ladies-in-waiting coveting the flowers, he muttered to Rose, "Fountain wants to see the snow globe. Did you bring it here with you? He says it sounds suspicious and he wants to work out the spell." Rose dug into her apron pocket. She was carrying it all the time now. She could have sworn it wanted her to. She felt oddly reluctant to hand it over to Freddie, though once she did, a strange chill seemed to leave her, her fingertips warming delightfully as Freddie tucked the tiny globe away. "Don't stare at it for too long," she muttered, feeling embarrassed.

Freddie looked at her sharply. "Like that, is it? Mr. Fountain said it sounded like some sort of entrapment as soon as I told him. Which wasn't soon enough, apparently. He was furious that I hadn't said anything before. Honestly, though, how was I supposed to know?" He glanced over at the audience and patted Rose's hand awkwardly. "Be careful, won't you? Here."

Quickly, he pulled out the watch chain and took the watch off, stuffing it clumsily into his jacket pocket.

"Have Gus. He might not stay, but I think you need him more than I do." He pressed the chain and the charms into Rose's hand, and Rose could feel the purring gold under her fingers.

Insolent boy! I'm not his to give! But I'll stay for a while, Gus yawned in her head. *Put me around your neck, Rose dear. I'll look after you. Do the princesses like fish?*

Twelve

ROSE DREAMED OF SNOWFLAKES falling and falling, settling on her face, blinding her eyes, sealing her nose and filling her mouth. They deadened her limbs with cold so she couldn't move, and she struggled helplessly, thrashing against her blankets, sure that they were a banked snowdrift into which she was sinking deeper and deeper. At last, she broke out of the snow and the dream at the same time and sat up gasping, rubbing frantically at her nose and eyes to clear away the choking snowflakes.

It was very cold, but there was no snow. In the faint light of a lamp that was burning in the princess's room, Rose examined her hands. Completely dry. A dream, then. Just a very real, horrible dream. She sighed shakily and lay down again, wriggling her frozen toes to try and warm them.

Then she sat up. The palace got colder at nights, when the fires died down, but never normally this cold. Her feet were actually aching it was so chilly. Something was wrong. And now she was paying proper attention, there was a strange rustling noise; she wasn't quite sure where. But usually the only noises were Princess Jane's very quiet, very little snores. Any noise was wrong.

Her heart suddenly frozen, by fear this time, Rose crawled out of bed and crept into Princess Jane's bedroom. The room was only dimly lit, but it was quite light enough to see that the bed was empty. Even so, Rose pulled off all the bedclothes—just in case the unbelievably serious little princess was playing a joke. Rose wasn't sure she even knew how.

Where is she? Gus was awake now, the little golden charm quivering against her neck.

I don't know! Rose wailed silently as she hurtled into the drawing room. The room was empty. "She's gone!" Rose whispered in horror.

"No." Gus came exploding out of his golden casing, tiny fragments of glittering metal shimmering into the air and coating his white fur, so that he gleamed as he tracked suspiciously round the room. "No, they're still here. They're hidden…"

All at once, as though they had realized they'd been discovered, there was a strange blurring in the air in front of Rose and Gus, and the room was suddenly so cold that Rose shivered, her limbs aching sharply and all her thoughts turning fuzzy and slow. Gus sprang into her arms, his gold-tinged fur filling her with blessed warmth, and she gasped in relief.

"Rose! Help me!" In the middle of the blur of figures was the princess, still kicking weakly as the kidnappers tried to carry her away. She was blue with cold, and as Rose stepped forward to help her, she seemed to faint. She had no magical cat to warm her against the ice spells.

Rose pulled at the black cloak of the nearest figure, desperately summoning as many of the fighting spells as she could. But there was no firelight to turn into a monster, and the deadening, blood-slowing cold made it hard to summon up any of the spells that she'd practiced on Freddie. Her mind seemed to be slowing down, her thoughts sticking together sluggishly.

Rose was too cold and frightened to think of anything clever. She ran straight into the muddle of figures and seized the hem of Princess Jane's nightgown.

There was an angry outcry from the dark figures, and someone hit her, knocking her sideways. A muffled oath sounded as Gus bit one of them, but the silken fabric on the nightgown was melting in Rose's hand like snowflakes, and then they were just gone.

All of them, Jane too. She was gone. Rose had failed entirely, but that wasn't what worried her. Who had taken Jane, and what were they going to do to her? The princess was selfish, rude, and monumentally tactless, but Rose *liked* Jane. And she was supposed to be responsible for her, and she was furious. Rose looked around, panicked, and grabbed the little bell that stood on one of the tables. Even that seemed to have been corrupted by the unnatural cold—it rang with a splintering tone like ice cracking and then crumbled to pieces.

Rose whirled around. Princess Jane had been taken. There was only one thing to do.

She screamed.

* * *

The princesses' suite was full of people. Rose sat on the window seat in the drawing room with Princess Charlotte in her arms. Gus was sitting on the child's lap, stoically allowing her to stroke his ears. The little princess was very confused and kept asking where Jane was in the most piteous fashion.

"She's gone away for the moment. She'll be back soon," Rose murmured for about the fifteenth time.

She didn't have the heart to be impatient with the little girl. It was Rose's fault that Jane was missing. She hid her face in Charlotte's dark curls for a moment, blinking away her tears. What should she have done?

"Rose!" Mr. Fountain was plunging across the room, courtiers hissing and whispering angrily as they saw him pass. He didn't even notice. "Are you hurt? Did they get to you too?"

Rose shook her head, her cheeks burning. She could hardly even look at him. "I was asleep," she whispered. "I heard something, and I ran after her and tried to fight, but it was no good. They were so strong. So cold. I could hardly move, and my mind felt like it was all locked up. What will they do to her?" She said this last in the merest thread of a whisper, breathing it around Charlotte so she didn't hear. It wasn't something she knew she could do, but she hardly noticed enough to be pleased with herself.

I don't know. Mr. Fountain spoke in her head. *It's safer this way. Did you see who they were?*

No! I'm so sorry. I just woke up because I was cold, and I heard something. Oh! Yes. The cold. It was magical; it had to have been. I had an awful dream—or I thought it was a dream… About snowflakes choking me. Maybe… that was a spell?

It sounds like it. Mr. Fountain's voice in her mind was grim. *I need to search for traces. Though how I'll get this lot out of here…*

The room was full of Princess Jane's ladies-in-waiting, all in tears, and about twenty other people, including the king and queen.

It was the first time that Rose had seen Queen Adelaide up close. She was stony-faced, clutching her little dog, but Rose wondered if the stone was to stop her collapsing. It reminded her of Jane. She couldn't look at the queen without feeling even guiltier.

"Where is Charlotte?" the queen asked suddenly, a rising panic in her voice.

Poor Charlotte seemed doomed always to be the afterthought. No one had asked about her before, since she stumbled shivering out of bed and into the middle of the maelstrom in her drawing room.

"She's here, Your Majesty." Mr. Fountain turned to reveal Rose and the little girl, and everyone in the room stared at them.

The queen looked as though she would like to snatch Charlotte out of Rose's arms. Rose tried to hold her out toward her mother, but Charlotte clung, her fingers biting into Rose's flesh.

Charlotte's mother rustled over in her full-skirted crepe-de-Chine dressing gown, frivolously patterned with poppies, and seated herself beside Rose on the window seat. Rose gulped. Her nightgown was touching the queen.

Mr. Fountain stepped back and bowed, but the queen ignored him.

"So you are my daughter's guard?" she asked. Her voice was as cold as the spell that had stolen Jane.

Rose nodded. "Yes, Your Majesty," she whispered to the floor.

"Did you do anything to stop this?" demanded the queen, leaning angrily close.

"I tried. They froze me," Rose repeated dully.

"Your Majesty." Mr. Fountain bowed very low again. "Rose did raise the alarm, immediately after the kidnap. The unnatural cold persisted in these rooms and still does. There may be traces that I can follow, but I need the room cleared."

Queen Adelaide stared at him with acute dislike. Rose realized that she really hated magic—which probably meant she was frightened of it. She had a feeling that the queen had not known what she really was until now—just another of her husband's strange whims.

The queen stood up and trailed her shimmering skirts over to where a group of courtiers were arguing—very, very politely—with the king. She spoke to him quietly, and he looked over at Mr. Fountain. "Everyone will leave," he said suddenly, a trace of hope in his voice, just for a moment. "We need to search the rooms."

"Sire, we have searched," a man in an ornate uniform began, "exhaustively. She is not here."

But the king waved them all out, and the queen followed, casting one last hateful glance at Rose and her master. Only the king was left, staring at Rose and Gus as they held his youngest daughter. Charlotte was falling asleep again on Rose's shoulder.

"There's a cat," he muttered, rather confused. "I didn't see it before."

"He's mine, sire," Mr. Fountain explained. "He was hidden and helping Rose. He is only almost a cat, sire, and very powerful, I promise you. This was an immensely strong spell, that neither Rose nor Gustavus were able to halt it."

The king watched Gus licking his paw, clearly trying to work out what "almost a cat" meant, and

Gus watched him around his bright pink tongue, his mixed eyes fixed on the king's face. Cats were allowed to be rude.

"Oh, Aloysius, what am I going to do?" he murmured, casting himself down next to Rose and burying his face in his hands. "It isn't just that she's my precious child. The political consequences!" He looked up, surprised, as Gus let out the merest breath of a growl. "Oh, I know, it seems cold. Ha! Stone cold! Frozen!" He shook his head dazedly, realizing that he was being criticized by a cat—realizing perhaps what "almost a cat" meant. "The banquet. For her birthday—tomorrow evening! And the Talish envoy coming, do you not see what that means?" He seemed to be talking to Gus, and the white cat stared back at him gravely. "A chance for a real peace, after all these years, all the ships and men we've lost at sea. They've lowered themselves to accept—we could hardly believe it—a banquet commemorating the night of the battle that lost them an empire. They must want peace." He looked pleadingly into Gus's amazing eyes. "Don't you see? If anyone outside the palace finds out that Jane is gone, there will be a national panic, and our chances of a lasting peace will be destroyed, perhaps forever."

"What will you do, sire?" Mr. Fountain asked.

"God knows…" The king shook his head. "It will all be ruined. There are elements in the Talish delegation who will frame it as an insult. They will go. Back to Talis to build more ships, more armies. I cannot let it happen, but I do not see any way to stop it!"

Mr. Fountain looked thoughtfully at Rose. "There is a way, sire…I objected to Rose being put at risk in this way at first, but as you say, the political consequences if the banquet should be canceled…So. There is a possible solution."

You can't make her do that! Gus snarled silently.

Mr. Fountain ignored him. "There has, after all, already been one unsuccessful attempt to steal the princess…"

The king blinked at him.

"We could tell everyone that this attempt was unsuccessful too." Mr. Fountain was still staring at Rose.

"We could replace the princess. Temporarily, of course," he added quickly. "Just until we find the real one. A stand-in…"

"How?" King Albert asked, his voice low and pained. Looking at him, the way his fingers were clenched, Rose had the sudden feeling that he was weighing the safety of his country against a deception that he hated with all his heart.

"A glamour." Rose held little Princess Charlotte tighter, and she squirmed and muttered in her sleep. She shook her head. "I can't do glamours. Remember when you tried to teach us? I made everyone's hair turn gold, but nothing happened to me. And Freddie and I practiced too, and it never worked right."

"With Gus and Freddie to help, Rose, you could. I will be chasing the real princess. I can feel the traces in here, and there must be some way I can track her. Sire, we must decide quickly, before these traces fade."

"Will you do this?" the king asked, peering wearily at Rose. He looked as though he hated to ask.

Rose gazed back at him. "She would want me to, I think. She complained about being a national treasure, but she was proud of it too. She would want the peace talks to go on." *If only because peace would mean disbanding some of the navy who keep sending her furniture,* she thought but didn't add.

"Gus, will you help her?" Mr. Fountain asked. The king gave the cat a sharp look, clearly surprised.

Gus gazed thoughtfully at Rose. "She could do it, no question. But should we?"

The king's mouth dropped open; then he shut it with a snap and swallowed. "You have a talking cat," he murmured. He shook his head. "I don't know why I'm surprised. Of course you do."

"Why is everyone always so impressed by the talking?" Gus inquired loftily. "It really isn't difficult." He headbutted the king on the arm. "I can do much more exciting things, you know."

"Jane adored cats," King Albert said quietly. "My wife wasn't keen—she has a dog. You will find her, won't you?" he asked Mr. Fountain suddenly. He didn't look at the magician, just kept stroking Gus under the chin, as though he couldn't bear to see Mr. Fountain's face.

Gus rubbed up against him again. "Do you really want an artificial daughter? That's what you're getting, you know. A replacement. Everyone else will think Rose is the real princess, and only you will know she's gone. Can you stand that, sire?" He placed a clawed paw on the king's arm. "I cannot let you risk Rose's life by betraying her." His strange eyes glowed. "She is as precious as your princess, and we cannot lose her."

The king gave a hollow laugh. "One gets rather good at pretending and giving up things one might want to do in order to promote the common good. I will treat her as my own child—and she will be under my protection."

Mr. Fountain nodded gravely, and Gus let out a solemn-sounding purr.

"Rose, can you lay the little princess down without waking her?" Mr. Fountain asked.

"No, give her to me." The king held out his arms, and Rose shuffled Charlotte onto his lap, where she snuggled sleepily. The king rubbed his bearded cheek against her hair for a mere fraction of a second, then looked up, all business. "How does this work? Can I watch? Is it a secret?"

Mr. Fountain shook his head. "No. You may watch, sire—you will not see a great deal of the spell anyway. You can help us if you think of Jane. We need to remember her as closely as we can, to make the glamour." He closed his eyes for a second. "I have called Freddie. His strength will be useful too."

Freddie arrived at a run a few minutes later, dressed only in shirt and breeches, his smooth hair ruffled and sticking out. It made him look nicer, Rose thought vaguely, trying to distract herself from what she was about to do.

Mr. Fountain had obviously told him what was about to happen in their telepathic speech, for he came straight to Rose and took her hands, staring at her anxiously. Then he remembered where he was and made a sketchy bow to the king, but he turned straight back to Rose. "Are you sure you want to do this? Disguise glamours are tricky, you know, and I don't mean just difficult. I mean tricky like they want to trick you."

"I have to," Rose said, shrugging and half nodding toward the king.

Freddie scowled. "He doesn't know what he's asking," he muttered. "I'm sorry, sire. But you don't. We would do anything to serve you, but this…this is above and beyond…"

Rose glanced worriedly at Mr. Fountain, and then back at Freddie. "Why? What's so special about it? When you first told me about glamours, you said they were difficult, that's all. Gus does them all the time, and it hasn't hurt him."

"They are difficult," Mr. Fountain agreed, steepling

his fingers thoughtfully. "And very, very strong magic. Which is why you'll need Freddie and Gus to help."

"Gus isn't human," Freddie argued, and Gus made a strange noise, half spit, half snarl. "Oh, all right, *mortal*. He's more than half magic already, Rose. It makes a big difference. If you use glamours too much, your humanity—felinity, then," he added as Gus's eyes sparked red, "it seeps away, and the magic leaks in to take its place." He sighed. "I'm not saying don't do it. I just mean be careful."

Rose nodded. "I will. Although seeing as I don't know what the spell is and I don't have any idea how it works, I don't see how I can help it if it leaks magic into me."

"Even knowing about it will help," Mr. Fountain promised. "Freddie was right to tell you. Some things I forget. The odd glamour, here and there, it all adds up. Who knows how much human I have left?" He laughed rather strangely, and everyone shivered. The king stared at him and unconsciously shuffled further back on the window seat, holding Princess Charlotte tighter.

Rose glanced at her master under her eyelashes. He seemed perfectly human to her. But then, supposing that was all just a glamour! What was he underneath? She stuffed the back of her hand into her mouth to stop herself squealing. She was being stupid. She'd seen glamours before, on Miss Sparrow, and she'd seen through them too, spotting the inconsistencies far better than Freddie could. Although, she had thought before that perhaps Mr. Fountain was rather good at them…

Rose shook herself. If the master were covered in glamours, surely he'd bewitch his mustache so he didn't have to sleep with it in a net and wax it with bear's grease every morning? And wasn't obsession with one's appearance a very human thing? A mostly magical creature wouldn't care if its mustache weren't perfectly pointy.

Besides, Rose didn't want to be Talish. She had nothing against the Talish particularly, although Bill swore they ate dormice, which seemed both cruel and unsanitary, but she liked being English, and eating porridge and kippers instead. If the peace efforts failed, and they went back to being at war with Talis, it was possible that they might lose—especially if the glorious power of the Royal Navy was disheartened by the loss of its princess. This spell was for the safety of the nation.

It was rather exciting when one thought of it like that.

"Help me with the spell," she asked, standing up with Gus in her arms. He gave a little mew of pleasure and excitement, and scrabbled his way onto her shoulders, coiling himself around so that his tail stroked one cheek and his whiskers the other. Rose shivered as she felt his magic surround her. It had never been so clear before, tiny pinpricks of magical dust falling and flickering into her skin. She could see Gus's luxuriant, powder-puff fur out of the corners of her eyes, and she suppressed a giggle. He might be a common tabby alley cat under all the magic. She would probably never know.

Freddie took her hands, still looking anxious, and she felt his magic pour into her skin, heating up her blood so that it raced around her body in a torrent of power and excitement. Rose bit her lip, not quite hard enough to draw that overheated blood out but close. She must keep herself under control. They hadn't even started the spell, and already she felt seduced by all that magic moving under her skin. She wondered if Mr. Fountain felt like this all the time, if perhaps she would when she was older and came into her full power. It made her all the more determined to make this work. She wanted to win, so that things could carry on as they were. So that she could grow up and learn to feel like this all the time.

Mr. Fountain began to whisper the spell—at least, it sounded like a whisper, but whispering was soft and quiet and gentle, and this noise was only as gentle as the tides, lapping against a beach, washing away the sand, eating through bare rock. It was a voice of true power, using all her master's magic and Freddie's and her own, with Gus's strange cat strength anchoring it all around Rose, as his body surrounded hers.

*Be the princess. In looks, in thought, in word, indeed.
In looks, in thought, in word, indeed.*

"Indeed," Freddie hissed.

Gus purred the word so that it buzzed through Rose's ears and seemed to echo round her skull. "Indeed…"

"Indeed," Rose added at last, completing the spell with her agreement and feeling her own flesh shudder and change.

Thirteen

ROSE LOOKED DOWN AT her own hands, and they weren't hers anymore. Her hands were small and bony, and the nails were cut short. There were rough bits round her knuckles from scrubbing coal dust away after laying the fires, and she had a scar from slicing the side of her left hand with a knife back in the kitchen at St. Bridget's, a long time ago.

These hands were even smaller, with long, delicate fingers and prettily kept nails, trimmed round and polished with a silken cloth by Lady Alice every morning. Princesses never nibbled their nails. The skin was white and soft, and a faint fragrance of roses came from the scented oil that was rubbed into the princess's skin.

It made Rose feel slightly sick.

"Go and look," Freddie said quietly. His face was serious and rather scared. He nodded toward a pretty filigree mirror that lay on a side table, its handle inlaid with turquoises and enameled with a *J*. "It's yours now," he whispered after her, and Rose turned around to glare at him.

"I'm not her! Don't you forget who I am, Frederick Paxton." Her voice sounded aristocratic. Royal. Not hers.

"You have to be her," Gus hissed in her ear, making Rose jump. She had forgotten for a moment that he was riding on her shoulders.

"But I'm me!" Rose protested, as she picked up the mirror. Then she looked into it and gulped. She wasn't her. She was a pretty, rather hard-faced little girl, with very smooth, light hair and pale eyes. At the moment, the girl looked worried, which was an unfamiliar expression on that face.

"If you think that, you'll be found out," the cat told her sternly, jumping from her shoulders back to the window seat and gently nosing at the king, who seemed frozen by the sight of Rose. "Jane has been learning to be a princess for almost eight years. We have about ten minutes before we'll have to tell everyone that you've been found."

"Won't I know how to be her?" Rose faltered. "Doesn't the glamour do that?"

"Only a little," Freddie explained. "A lot of it is just acting."

"Oh…" Rose laid the mirror back down and walked slowly round the room, trying to feel like a princess. She picked up one of the dollhouse dolls that had been left lying on the floor and put it back into the house, setting it on a tiny silken sofa and arranging its twisted limbs in a delicate pose.

"Well, don't do that for a start!" Gus snapped.

"Princesses do not tidy up. They have people like you to do that."

"Yes…" Rose shut the dollhouse's front distractedly and nodded. What *did* Jane do? She had lessons, and she played. She was rather like a doll herself, with all the dressing and undressing, and polishing and brushing. "I suppose if I've just been kidnapped again, that might give me a little leeway, don't you think? I could be rather confused? Won't that give me an excuse for anything I do wrong?"

King Albert blinked his way out of a stupor, stuck staring at this witch child, and nodded. "Yes. Jane was confused when it happened last time." He shook his head, clearly trying not to think what might be happening to his real daughter right now. "You look so like her," he whispered sadly, his voice cracking.

"Jane!" Unnoticed, little Princess Charlotte had woken up and was stretching out her arms to her sister. "They said you'd gone again, Jane, but I knew you wouldn't, because you didn't like it last time. You said so."

Everyone flinched.

Princess Charlotte slid down from her father's lap and went to Rose, who was staring at her rather as one would look at a snake. Rose stopped herself from stepping back and returned Charlotte's hug when the little girl put her arms out. She had been holding

189

her before, so why did it feel so wrong now? She gave Freddie and Gus an agonized look, and the cat jumped down from the window seat to brush lovingly against Charlotte's legs.

Charlotte chuckled. "Oh, he's pretty." But she gave Rose a strange look as she bent down to stroke Gus. She seemed to know something wasn't quite right.

The king stood up and touched Charlotte gently on the cheek. He looked at Rose and tried to do the same to her, lifting his hand, but he couldn't quite bring himself to touch her. "Frederick, please explain to the princess's ladies that she has returned, though we are not sure how. Tell them that your master is trying to find out what has happened, and they should attend upon Her Highness in her bedchamber in a little while, when she has had time to recover herself."

"What do I do now?" Rose asked, reaching out to touch his arm as he made for the door, but she didn't quite dare to grab his sleeve and he hurried away. Rose sighed and dropped onto the window seat. "I suppose I recover myself, whatever that means."

Freddie came back in and stood staring at her, as though she was absolutely fascinating. "Stop it," Rose snapped.

"That's better," Gus told her approvingly. "Much more royal."

"Sorry," Freddie murmured. "You look just like her. It's uncanny."

"I'm meant to!" Rose said crossly. "That was the whole point."

Princess Charlotte, meanwhile, had vanished back into her own bedchamber, which opened off the drawing room like her sister's. She came back carrying a large book hugged to her front and looking hopeful. "Jane, will you read me a story? Please?" She gazed at what she thought was her sister and frowned again, just a little.

"Freddie, come and help me search," Mr. Fountain called. He was examining the carpet on his knees with a monocle.

"What is that man doing?" Princess Charlotte asked, her eyes wide.

"He's looking for magic," Rose told her, trying to sound like a big sister. "To see if he can find who it was who cast the spell that took me."

"Where did you go?"

Rose sighed. "I honestly don't know." It was true after all. "Let's go and read this book."

"Oh, yes. It's your favorite," Charlotte promised. "Can the lovely cat come too?"

Gus twitched his whiskers graciously and led the way into Princess Jane's room. They settled themselves on Jane's bed, the silken sails forming a tent all around them that felt safe and warm. Rose looked out of the corner of her eye at her own bed, just visible through the door, and wished she was back in it, fast asleep.

The book was a treasury of fairy tales, hand-colored

and ornamented with gold leaf around the capitals. Rose couldn't help stroking it admiringly, until Charlotte pulled at her sleeve. "Read it! Please," she added, as an afterthought.

Rose embarked on the tale of the Frog Prince, although she was rather distracted from the story and kept losing her place.

They got as far as the princess allowing the frog into the palace and grudgingly allowing him to eat from her golden plate, which Princess Charlotte pronounced disgusting. Then she looked up at Rose, staring sternly into her eyes. "Who are you?" she asked. She was quite polite but obviously determined to have a proper answer.

Rose looked down at her, open-mouthed, and even Gus laid his ears back.

"You aren't my sister," Charlotte stated firmly. "She never does voices when she reads out loud, and she hates this book. She says the stories are all boring and stupid and wrong, and she won't read it ever, ever again. But *you* didn't even complain when I gave it to you."

"Tell her," Gus said grimly.

Princess Charlotte gasped. She had been asleep when Gus was talking before, and now her eyes opened wide and she gazed at him in wondering admiration. "Oh, a talking cat!"

Gus rolled his eyes irritably.

"You're right," Rose told her. "I'm just under a spell to look like Jane. Because she has to go to this big dinner tomorrow, and it would be awful for the country if she missed it."

"But where is she?" Charlotte asked. She was still looking at Gus, not Rose, but there was a note in her voice that suggested she very much wanted the answer to this question.

Rose took a deep, careful breath. She didn't want a screaming four-year-old, although an argument might be the best way to convince everyone that she and Charlotte were really sisters.

"She was taken by a spell. That's why Mr. Fountain is in the drawing room. He's trying to work out who did it."

"And you're really Jane's new maid, aren't you?" Charlotte pointed out smugly.

Rose nodded. "I'm actually Mr. Fountain's apprentice."

"Oh, I see. So that's why you have a magical cat." Charlotte nodded to herself, pleased to have this mystery solved. She placed a little white hand on Rose's slightly larger white hand. "Mr. Fountain is very clever, isn't he? He will find Jane, won't he?"

"I hope so," Rose muttered. Then she added, trying to sound more confident, "Oh, yes, I'm sure he will."

Charlotte leaned back against her supposed sister's shoulder again and pointed to the book. "You were here," she said firmly.

Rose gave a little gasping laugh and carried on reading. It was a beautiful story and funny, and keen to distract the little princess and herself, she let her mind wander among the wonderful pictures, until Gus hissed a warning in her ear, and Princess Charlotte cried out delightedly.

"Oh no, don't stop it! Look, he's going to turn into the prince! The book never did that before." She wriggled closer, so that her nose was practically touching the page, and Rose watched in horror as the frog in the painted illustration stretched and grew and turned into a rather beautiful young man with no clothes on and a discreetly positioned hot water bottle. The princess in the picture looked very shocked and so was Rose, but Princess Charlotte laughed and laughed. "I can see his *bottom*!" she giggled, obviously finding this hysterically funny.

Gus put one plump white paw over the offending part and ran the claws of the other paw into Rose's arm, but only a little way. "Be careful!" he hissed crossly.

"How did it do that?" Rose murmured, hardly noticing. "I don't even know this story. I didn't tell it to do that!"

"So I should hope," Gus sniffed disapprovingly. "I should think the artist who painted it knew the tale though, and perhaps others have read the book and thought about things they shouldn't have. You just— er—brought them out, shall we say…"

A frog who turned back into a prince probably wouldn't have any clothes on, Rose admitted, trying not to look at her embarrassing magic. Then she shook herself crossly, stared hard at the thick, smooth paper, and scowled. A large and rather too modern wardrobe appeared at the back of the picture (Rose was in too much of a hurry to think about accuracy here), the painted princess threw her dressing gown at the frog prince (who still had very pale green skin, Rose noted interestedly) and he shrugged it on and bolted for the wardrobe, pulling out a horrible, gaudy outfit in a garish shade of green (which was Rose's revenge). He glared at her out of the page but put it on obediently.

"Yes, he should wear green always, to remind him of being a frog." Princess Charlotte nodded approvingly. "Can he have a hat, please?"

The prince plucked a hat with a long acid-green feather from one of the bedposts and put it on, bowing to both princesses. Then the book shut, all by itself, with a snap.

"That was the best story I've ever heard." Princess Charlotte sighed with satisfaction.

"Your Highness!" Lady Alice came running into the room—or would have done if she had ever done anything as unladylike as run. "What happened? Where did you go?"

Rose looked frantically at Gus, who shrugged

elegantly and most unhelpfully, and shook his shimmery whiskers.

"I don't know. I can't remember. It was all misty…" Rose hoped that this bore some relation to what Princess Jane had said about the last time; she had never dared to ask her.

Lady Alice was distracted anyway, as she had noticed Gus nestling on the princess's pillow. "Where did that animal come from?" she asked in a shocked voice. She was very much the queen's creature and disliked cats on principle.

The fur stood up on Gus's back, and his eyes darkened to indigo and amber. Rose could feel him vibrating with fury, and she spoke quickly. "Oh, he is a present from Mr. Fountain, Lady Alice! As an apology, because that strange girl, Rose, whom he recommended to Papa has had to leave. Some problem with her—with her family." It was hard to say that, but it sounded right, and she knew that Lady Alice had had her suspicions of the unknown servant-companion that had been foisted on her princess.

"Oh, really!" Lady Alice's eyes brightened at the news. "Well, that is quite typical. She seemed a most unreliable girl. I always said so."

Rose smiled. As she remembered it, Lady Alice had been quite happy to shuffle off some of her duties onto the unreliable girl, but she nodded anyway. "And now we have this dear cat instead." She made her voice very firm. No one was going to suggest taking Gus away.

Gus settled his fur back down but glared at Lady Alice, his tail twitching slightly.

"Well, of course, if Your Highness is fond of him…" the lady-in-waiting murmured doubtfully.

"Very fond. I find him quite delightful, and I shall be keeping him," Rose said airily, trying to sound like Jane at her most regal.

Flattery always worked on Gus, and he preened himself happily, purring at Lady Alice, who gave a thin smile. "Dear little kitty…" she said in a most unconvincing voice, and Rose tried very hard not to laugh. How on earth did Jane manage it? Perhaps she didn't find all this as funny as Rose did—or perhaps she just didn't know any different.

* * *

Luckily, being kidnapped by magic meant that everyone was very sympathetic to Rose, and no one made her do lessons for the next two days, which was fortunate, as Princess Jane was extremely accomplished and knew all sorts of tricky dates. Rose had inquired of Gus whether he and Freddie could make her fluent in Talish to cope with Jane's terrifying governess, Miss Plaidy. (She was Scottish. No one wanted the princess to have an actual Talish governess, as it would be politically rather difficult, but knowledge of Talish was seen as very important, particularly when one didn't trust the Talish one inch.) Gus had yawned and said, somewhat unconvincingly, that he wished he could help, but magic didn't really work like that, as it was regarded as cheating. Some things had to be done by proper hard work. Rose wasn't sure if this was true or if he just wanted to keep her busy. But by looking pale and occasionally staring into the distance (usually because she was trying to work out what Jane would have said or done), Rose managed to make everyone think she was feeling delicate. The ladies-in-waiting reacted to this by not letting her lift so much as a teacup and fanning her every so often. It was so important that Jane was well and in good looks for the banquet that Rose was allowed to spend two days mostly on a sofa with her eyes closed, which was perfect, because she could manage to look like Jane, but behaving like her was full of pitfalls.

Princess Charlotte, luckily, seemed rather pleased to have a secret, although she did keep dropping rather frightening hints, and Rose had to bribe her with sugared almonds, doled out one by one from a supply procured by Freddie. Her supposed sister had a particular weakness for the pink ones, and Rose rather liked them too, though not as much as her favorite chocolate satins. She had to eat them secretly though, as it was well-known that the princess did not have a sweet tooth.

The accuracy of Rose's glamour was thoroughly tested the next afternoon, when Jane's dress for the banquet was brought for its final alterations. The princesses had their own seamstress, and she had clearly been working on this creation for a long while.

"I can't think what's happened," she muttered anxiously, as she slit a seam to let the bodice out, carefully unpicking the threads so as not to shred the crystal embroidery that covered the pale pink silk in flowery swirls. "I'm so sorry, Your Highness. I was sure it fitted perfectly last week. But there's a good half an inch needed between those fastenings."

"Too many sugared almonds," Gus murmured very quietly from behind the curtains, and Rose scowled at him over her shoulder while trying not to move for fear of being pinned. He was quite capable of speaking to her silently, but he liked to court discovery by whispering. Lady Alice kept almost catching him and giving him the most worried looks. He watched her meaningfully whenever she was in the same room, which meant she tried to stay away from him, which Rose found very useful.

"Will you be able to finish it in time?" Rose asked.

"Oh, yes, yes, of course, Princess Jane!" Miss Bullerby was on her knees anyway, tugging at the silk as though she thought it might have got caught up somewhere, and the missing half an inch was going to miraculously reappear. But the pose made her look remarkably like she was begging for mercy. It was horrid, and Rose had to resist putting out a hand and hauling her up.

"I promise you, it will be perfect for tonight. I shall go and do it now. It will be perfect!" She stared up at Rose, her mouth full of pins, and her eyes wide with panic.

"I didn't mean…" Rose trailed off, realizing that Jane probably *would* have meant it that way. Her seamstress had made a mistake (one that was rather unflattering), and she would expect it to be sorted out at once. Rose had been feeling sorry for Miss Bullerby, as she knew quite well that she and Mr. Fountain and Freddie and Gus had just misremembered how plump Jane was around the ribs. She fell silent and sucked her stomach in as much as she could to be helpful.

"Don't do that," Gus breathed. "You have to wear that dress for a three-hour banquet tonight. You need room."

Rose grimaced. Despite the fact that she was being fitted with a dress for the banquet, she was trying not to think about it. It was all very well spending the last two days reclining on the sofa, but she had to be a princess tonight. A princess who was the center of attention and, horror of horrors, actually had to make a speech.

Miss Bullerby disappeared with an armful of pink silk and a haunted expression, leaving Rose to the mercy of the hairdresser. She had had to wear curling papers all day and was desperate to take them out, but the sight of a basketful of pink rosebuds and a tray of skewering hairpins was not exactly encouraging.

Gus leaped into her lap as she sat down in front of the dressing table mirror, and Charlotte dragged up a pretty gilt stool, which looked as though it might not have been made by a sailor.

"Are you going to put Ro…" Charlotte trailed off and giggled. "*Jane's* hair up, Miss Trout?"

"Half up, Princess Charlotte. Ringlets down the back and woven with rosebuds. Her Majesty thinks you're still too young to wear it up all the way."

Rose nodded. It made the roots of her hair ache, and she shot a warning glare at Charlotte, who smirked knowingly. She knew her secret was important and mustn't be told, but she adored having it, and she couldn't help teasing about it every so often. Rose bit her lip, looking at herself—her temporary self—in the mirror. Charlotte was still only a four-year-old, even though she was an incredibly grown-up little girl. It would be so easy for her to forget and just blurt the secret out.

Rose hadn't seen Mr. Fountain since the day before, when she'd left him inspecting her carpet. She supposed he wouldn't usually meet Princess Jane, but she hated not knowing what was going on, whether he'd come any closer to finding her. Freddie had been no use at all when he crept into the suite that morning, trying to dodge the ladies-in-waiting, whom he said gave him the shivers.

He'd shaken his head when Rose asked for news, shrugging helplessly. "It's all tied in with the winter magic, he's sure of that. And he thinks it's more than one person, a lead magician with a gang of helpers. Very organized. But he hasn't got any further than that yet. He's exhausted, Rose. He's been trying so hard."

Lady Alice had returned just then and glared disapprovingly at this boy in her princesses' rooms. And a boy who was one of those untrustworthy magicians as well…Freddie had been forced to pretend to be teaching Rose to disappear an egg, and the egg had most unfortunately broken all over the sofa. Freddie had left in disgrace, and since then Rose and Gus had had no news at all.

Now, in the middle of the hairdressing, Gus's back stiffened suddenly, his whiskers trembled, and he turned on Rose's lap to look up at her with deep excitement in his eyes and, disconcertingly, a tiny hint of fear. *He's found them!* he told Rose, his thoughts humming with excitement and his paws kneading her skirt compulsively. *They're still in the palace. I don't believe it. He doesn't know who they are, but he can feel they're here.*

Rose felt her fingers clench into little claws of panic. She hadn't considered before what the kidnappers must be thinking. There was someone else who knew she was an impostor. What if they came back for her? Her heart thudded painfully and she looked from side to side, instinctively trying to guard herself.

"Your Highness! Please don't twitch like that!" No one would ever snap at Princess Jane, of course, but Miss Trout came awfully close, as Rose nearly ruined her hairstyle.

"I'm sorry," Rose muttered through her teeth, trying to breathe calmly, her fingers tangling in Gus's fur until he hissed disapprovingly. *Stop that! We will not let them hurt you. You're safe.*

Rose looked down at him doubtfully, but his strange mixed eyes glowed with confidence and love. She stroked him gratefully, feeling the strong magic from his fur pulsing through her fingers and deep into her heart. She had never felt so clearly that Gus did love her, for he was a sarcastic, grumpy creature, with a wicked sense of humor, and he didn't like to make his deeper feelings known.

"There!" Miss Trout stood back proudly. Rose looked up at herself in the mirror and smiled to protect Miss Trout's feelings. She didn't feel like smiling; it was still too odd to look at her reflection and not be her. But Jane's hair did look pretty. It had been almost worth the curl papers.

Miss Trout and Lady Alice buttoned Rose into the complicated petticoats—edged with crystals to match the dress—and Miss Bullerby brought the dress back, looking worriedly at Rose in case she'd managed to grow another inch around since the last fitting. Oddly enough, it now seemed slightly too big, and Gus admitted silently to Rose that he had tried to adjust the glamour and might have exaggerated slightly. Still, the sash pulled it in, and only Miss Bullerby would notice. She kept staring at Rose's waist and muttering to herself while Lady Alice arranged the princess's magnificent rose pearls.

"Your father was so clever to find you these for your birthday," she murmured admiringly. "And to give them to you in advance so the dress could match them. Inspired."

Rose had never had a birthday present, as she didn't know when her birthday was, but she couldn't help feeling that she would have preferred a surprise on the actual day. Charlotte had been begging her to open the pile of presents in the drawing room all day, but she was supposed to wait until after the banquet, which seemed to be her official birthday. It was all very grand and rather cold. But the pearls almost made her consider staying a princess. She had never seen anything so lustrous, and they felt alive against her skin. She was sure that her cheeks grew pinker when she put them on, and they didn't feel magical.

She was still admiring them when the page boy scratched at the door to ask if he could admit Freddie and Bella. Lady Alice tried to say no, but Rose ran into the drawing room without listening and threw her arms round Freddie.

"Don't!" he muttered, wriggling away. "Jane would never do that. Rose, let go!"

"What are you doing here? Have you got news? Gus says Mr. Fountain's found them!" Rose asked, leading them to the window seat and beckoning Charlotte to come too. Lady Alice hovered by the door with her lips pursed.

Freddie cast a doubtful glance at Charlotte, and Rose put an arm around her little sister. "She worked it out."

"She's kept the secret," Gus agreed in a purring whisper, rubbing his head against Charlotte's stockings. "She should be allowed to hear what's going on."

Freddie nodded. "We don't know anything more. We're only here because Bella's father said we should come and help you keep up the glamour. He thinks with everyone staring at you tonight, it will wear down faster and you'll need us to stop it slipping."

"Slipping?" Rose asked in a sharp voice, imagining Jane's features sliding down her face and leaving her own nose bare underneath. "What does that mean?"

Freddie shrugged and looked at Bella. "You'd just start to look more like you. Your hair would get dark again to start with, probably."

"In the middle of the banquet!" Rose moaned faintly.

"No, silly, because we won't let it," Bella told her in a no-nonsense voice that Rose suspected she'd learned from Miss Bridges. "Papa is starting to suspect that I can use my magic after all, and so—"

"Starting to suspect!" Freddie scoffed. "He knows, Bella. Miss Bridges told him you levitated Susan!"

"Oh, well done!" Rose said gratefully.

Bella stared at the ceiling with a saintly expression on her face. "Susan tripped and most unfortunately fell down the stairs," she recited, as though she had said it several times before. Then she glanced wickedly at Rose. "Strangely, just after she'd called me a spoiled little princess. Sorry…" she added, looking at Charlotte.

Charlotte only giggled. "I wish you could teach me to do that."

"She wasn't hurt, was she?" Rose asked, feeling a little guilty.

"No, but the tea service is coming out of her wages, and it was the Meissen," Bella gloated.

"Oh, Bella!" Rose protested. "It's so pretty, and it was a complete set!"

"It isn't now." Bella sniggered. "Oh, come on, Rose, Susan's horrid to you. Why are you fussing?"

"It just doesn't seem fair," Rose muttered. "She's scared of magic, that's why she's so mean."

Bella sniffed. "So she should be. Stop being feeble. Are you ready for tonight? We can't sit very near you, but Papa says you should at least be able to see us." She sighed. "There wasn't time to have a new dress made, and this velvet is old."

Bella was wearing a wonderful green and gold dress that Rose had never seen before. It was almost as rich as her own, with its seed pearl collar.

"You need to be going down to the Cascade Hall now, Your Highness." Lady Alice bustled over importantly.

Rose gave Freddie a panicked look and jumped as something tiny ran up her sleeve. She thought for a moment of horror that it was a mouse, but then Gus spoke in her mind. *Don't hit me! I'm hiding in your sleeve. You'll need me there, and I don't think even Princess Jane could get away with taking me to a state banquet.*

Rose peeped up her sleeve under the guise of checking for her handkerchief and smiled at the tiny, finger-length white cat clinging to her deep lace cuff. *I didn't know you could do that.*

The world is full of things you don't know, dear Rose. Good luck. And don't wave at anyone.

Fourteen

THE CASCADE HALL WAS a new addition of the king's, which Freddie and Bella had told Rose about. She had a vague idea of what it would be like, but even the grandeur of the public corridors hadn't been anything like this. Rose could understand why Mr. Fountain made rude remarks about the palace being gaudy and tasteless, but this room full of sparkling light and water took the breath out of her mouth, and for half a second she forgot she was an artificial princess and simply stared.

"Her Royal Highness, Princess Jane!" a liveried butler roared, and Lady Alice nudged her forward.

Gulping down her fear, which had returned with a rush, Rose fixed on a royal sort of smile and walked slowly toward the top table, where Gus had warned her she would be sitting.

Luckily there was some excuse for her wide-eyed look. The centerpiece of the room, now arranged with a horseshoe of tables surrounding it, was a miniature waterfall, cascading into a mother-of-pearl pool, surrounded by tiny, jeweled trees. And in honor of the princess's birthday, the water had been dyed a delicate pink.

The king and queen were waiting for her, and her three older sisters. Rose hoped she didn't have to talk to them. They were so similar, she was sure she would call them by the wrong names. The king smiled fixedly at Rose and led her toward a small, rather plump man, with amazingly white teeth and a scarlet silk waistcoat adorned with hummingbirds. Across the waistcoat ran a blue sash covered in sparkling medals and orders. He was talking animatedly to the gang of courtiers around him, but when Rose approached, he bowed to her deeply.

"Your Highness. My country is most sensible of the honor you do us with this kind invitation to your— little party." He waved a delicate hand, somehow managing to include the cascade and the throng of glittering guests in this strange description.

"Jane, this is Lord Venn, the Talish envoy." The king's voice was tense and low.

Rose curtseyed back, looking at him under her eyelashes and noting how he in turn was watching the king, trying to see whether he'd succeeded in upsetting the man he was supposed to be courting for the emperor. Rose began to feel that the Talish envoy might not actually be as keen on a peace agreement as everyone thought.

Lord Venn took her hand and lifted it to his lips.

Rose repressed a shudder of distaste but couldn't stop a sharp intake of breath as he touched her skin. She could feel the magic running around him, a sour fizzing that made her hand sting. She forced herself to smile, instead of snatching back her hand. Could he tell that she too was a magician? No one had mentioned to her that he was. Did they not know?

Rose tried to look around for Freddie and Bella as she listened politely to the stream of flowery compliments that the Talish envoy was addressing to her. She spotted them at last, standing together halfway down the room, but she couldn't catch their eyes.

Gus, did you know he was a magician? she asked anxiously.

No, and neither did the master, Gus snapped back. *You need to concentrate.*

Lord Venn was looking at her rather oddly, and Rose smiled sweetly at him. He had been speaking in English, but his accent was strong and she hadn't understood it all. Smiling seemed the safest thing to do. She made herself listen more carefully now, desperate not to insult him by accident. This banquet was so important. She'd gone through this whole charade for the sake of the next few hours. She felt as though she owed it to Jane to do it properly. Politely, she asked Lord Venn if he had any children. She knew quite well that he did; Lady Alice had told her so she could use them in conversation.

As the envoy enthused to her about the beauty of his little girls, the king and queen decided to sit down, so of course everyone else did too. Lord Venn and his entourage sat opposite Rose and her parents, but luckily the king and queen didn't seem to expect her to do more than smile.

He keeps staring at me! Rose thought urgently to Gus. *Don't you think so?*

The tiny cat was now hiding in the little arrangement of pink flowers next to Rose's plate, and he peered cautiously around a rose.

Yes. And you haven't done anything wrong, wonder of wonders. Yet.

Can he see the glamour if he's a magician? Rose asked.

He shouldn't be able to. Not unless…

What?

Unless he already had some reason to suspect you…

He knows, Rose told him, crumpling her napkin.

You could be right, Gus conceded.

A page served her a portion of salmon—which had Gus leaning most incautiously out of the roses—and Rose was hidden from Lord Venn for a moment. She seemed able to think better without those strange sparkling medals filling her eyes and distracting her from looking at him properly. He was definitely suspicious, and if Gus, ever critical, said she hadn't betrayed herself, then she believed him.

In which case, the envoy had been suspicious

before—which meant he already knew she wasn't the real princess.

Rose stabbed a golden fork into the salmon unseeingly, not even caring if she'd picked up the correct one from the array of seven or so at the side of her plate.

She was sitting across the table from Jane's kidnapper.

The salmon tasted of nothing. Rose pushed it around her plate, and Gus watched it sadly. What should she do? She couldn't possibly stand up and accuse the Talish envoy of kidnapping the princess. Even if it were true, it would cause the most enormous diplomatic upset, the sort of thing Freddie worried about his cousin Raphael doing. And what if she were wrong? It didn't bear thinking about.

Rose wished her magic was strong enough to talk silently to Freddie and Bella and ask for help, but she could only do it when she was speaking to someone very close—to the other side of the room, she had no chance. Gus was too taken up with the salmon, a tiny piece of which he'd hooked when no one was looking, and he would probably balk at relaying messages for her anyway. Rose stared desperately at Freddie, hoping to make him look at her, but he was looking at his plate and listening to something Bella was telling him.

The glamour! Of course. She had Freddie and Bella's magic tied to hers. Thinking hard, Rose wrapped a finger into one of her glamoured curls and twisted, calling them. *Look at me! Freddie!*

Freddie sat up sharply and stared at her, then in response to her frown, pretended to be looking at the waterfall.

What's the matter?

It's Lord Venn! He's a magician, and he stole Jane, I'm almost sure. What do I do?

Freddie looked at Bella helplessly, and Bella gave a tiny shrug at Rose. They hadn't planned for this.

Rose's job had been to keep the banquet going, not to disrupt it with news of a dangerous plot.

What does Gus think? Freddie asked at last, and Rose felt Gus join the conversation, yawning, sated with salmon.

Gus thinks he's a dangerous lunatic and the middle of a state banquet is not the moment to expose him. Wait until afterward. Ask to speak to the king. It is your birthday, after all.

Rose nodded very slightly. Wait. That was best. She picked halfheartedly at her duck with cherries and tried to listen to the king and Lord Venn carefully discussing the state of the navy.

Rose's napkin was a bedraggled rag from twisting it over and over by the time four small pages appeared carrying an enormous pink birthday cake. It had four tiers, crusted with frills and swags of pink and white and silver icing, and garlands of pink sugar roses. Eight candles sat around the top tier in silver holders, and the pages abandoned it gratefully in front of Rose.

Lord Venn applauded, clapping his plump hands

delicately, and smiled around at Rose and the king and queen. "Charming, charming! My dear princess, after you have cut your cake, you must honor me by opening a special present that we have brought with us from the emperor." He looked questioningly at the king, who agreed with a gracious nod.

The plump little man beamed and chuckled as Rose sliced into the first tier of the cake with a silver knife, but his smile chilled Rose. He didn't mean it, not even as much as any jaded diplomat pandering to a spoiled princess. It was all a sham, she was sure. They wanted something, and she didn't know what. The cake tasted like dust in her mouth, dry and powdery and sickly sweet, but she forced it down, smiling as hard as the traitor on the other side of the table. She had only one advantage in this game: that he did not know she had discovered him. She had to keep up the pretense.

At last she had eaten it, and the Talish envoy was rising to speak, his waistcoat swelling like a fat pigeon. He beckoned to one of his aides to bring the present, and Rose heard not a word of his flowery speech. Holding the gold-wrapped gift, trailing yards of ribbons and flowers, was someone she knew—a tall, thin, white-faced man with colorless hair and ice-blue eyes. A man who had given her a present already. The man who had made the snow globes.

Rose! Freddie was calling her urgently. *Don't open it!*

But the present was in her hands now, paraded to

her by the page boys, and everyone was watching. She had to open it!

She glanced worriedly at the king, trying to signal what was going on, trying to explain why she hadn't started to untie the golden ribbons, but he only frowned and gestured toward the parcel.

I know it's a spell. A trick. I can open it carefully and not let it do whatever it's supposed to. Then everyone will see what's going on, Rose reasoned to herself, the thoughts flitting in a panic through her mind as she undid the first bow. *Because I can feel him getting angry, and if I don't open it, something awful is going to happen. He doesn't care who he hurts…*

She could feel the magician on the other side of the table, his heart beating even faster than her own, his defenses slipping as he waited for the spell to begin.

Slowly, still trying to smile, as though she really were an excited child opening a present, Rose folded back the golden paper, revealing a jeweled box.

"How pretty," she said politely, glancing across the table.

"Open it, Your Highness," Lord Venn said, his smile showing more and more of his teeth.

What is he trying to do? Rose wondered, as she lifted the heavy golden lid. *If he knows I'm not the princess, because he already has her, what does he want from me? Does he want to steal me too? What on earth for?* She imagined for a lunatic second a collection of princesses in glass cases. The golden hinges of the box wheezed open slowly, revealing a little golden bird, each feather exquisitely inlaid with colored enameling and gemstones.

"Ohh…" Rose itched to touch it, to stroke the enamel feathers, but she knew she mustn't. What if these magicians had coated it in poison, to kill her out of revenge for spoiling their plan? Although, why? She still couldn't see why, if they knew she wasn't the real princess, they didn't just tell everyone. Perhaps they thought no one would believe such a silly story.

"Do you like it, Princess?" Lord Venn purred, and Rose nodded, finding it easier to smile at him this time—the bird was so beautiful, even if it was a trick.

"Watch…" The envoy's little black eyes sparkled with a hard light, like diamonds—like the bird's eyes, though they were wonderful fiery rubies, glittering in golden eyelids.

There was a strange clicking noise from the box, and the bird, which had been lying on its side with its head tucked down on its breast, looked up at Rose. She jumped back against her chair in shock, but the little creature stood up in its box and turned its head from side to side, as though it were surveying the gathering. Then it turned back to Rose, the ruby eyes staring fixedly at her.

Rose felt a strange crawling feeling running down her spine. The bird was beautiful but eerie. The ruby eyes glowed, and they seemed to hold her still. She couldn't look away. The bird hopped out of the box, its diamond claws scratching at the linen tablecloth, and stalked toward her, hopping in a rather ungainly fashion, like a real bird, not designed for being on the ground. It stopped at the edge of the tablecloth and turned its head from side to side, staring at her with those bright ruby eyes.

"How very beautiful," Queen Adelaide commented, smiling as her older daughters admired the creature with well-trained compliments. "Does it sing, Lord Venn?"

The envoy bowed slightly, glancing toward the queen for only a second. "I am afraid not, Your Majesty. It does—other things…"

The cut-glass tones of Jane's mother had roused Rose from the strange trance the bird had led her into. She blinked frantically and looked for Gus.

The tiny cat—who was even smaller than the bird—was still perched among the roses, his eyes fixed on it hungrily.

Remember you're shrunk! Rose told him quickly, as it looked as though he were about to pounce.

On the edge of the table, the bird shook out its wings in a flurry of golden feathers, and the court clapped in admiration. The sudden noise seemed to shock the glittering creature, and it fluttered and hopped in panic, its head twitching, before it returned to gazing at Rose. It was amazingly real, she thought. It reminded her of the sparrows that occasionally perched around the little window in her attic bedroom, though they were poor dusty cousins of this magnificent creature. And it was bigger, of course, the size of a fat blackbird.

It stretched out its wings again, clearly about to fly, and the assembled guests held their breath, not wanting to scare the creature once more.

Rose bit her lip worriedly. She had resolved not to touch the bird—it was clearly magical, and it must be enchanted to attack her somehow. But if it could fly… As she thought it, the golden bird sprang into the air with the ease of one of those grubby little sparrows and landed on her pink silk sleeve.

Everyone gasped, and the bird gave a strange mechanical chirrup and took off again—but this time, the diamond claws were fixed fast in Rose's dress; she could feel them starting to dig into her skin too, making her scream as they cut through her flesh. Jane's older sisters cried out in sympathy, and King Albert shoved his chair back angrily, pushing it over.

"Stop it! It's hurting her!" The queen stood up. "It's going wrong. Make it stop!"

Rose pulled frantically away, but the tiny creature was incredibly strong, and it was starting to pull her out of her chair. Several of the guards, the princesses, and even Lady Alice tried to wave the bird away, but it pecked them viciously with its enameled yellow beak, leaving bleeding gouges across their hands.

Across the table, Lord Venn showed his teeth in a shining grin, clapping his hands together lightly as he watched his creation work. Several of his entourage had moved in closer and surrounded him, revealing what they really were—his bodyguards.

"Do you not like the gift, Your Highness?" he asked, his voice humming sweetly.

"Stop this! Tell whoever is controlling this evil creature to stop it! Or I will have it shot!" the king shouted, his hands clenching as he watched Rose fighting the creature.

"I wouldn't," Lord Venn told him silkily. "You would miss. And who knows what the bullet would hit? The princess, perhaps? And that might be unfortunate for you, Your Majesty. A glamour only works while the creator is alive, you know. Perhaps Aloysius Fountain failed to tell you that. No matter. Whoever this child is, we will see her real face when she dies. Which should be soon—when my little bird carries her up to the ceiling and drops her down again."

Everyone involuntarily glanced up toward the vaulted ceiling, with its glowing chandeliers. Rose was standing now, pulled onto tiptoes by the bird's straining wings. She batted at it frantically, and it pecked her.

"What is he talking about?" the queen demanded, throwing her arms around Rose's waist to hold her down. "Help me!"

"Look! Look at her!" Lord Venn gloated. "She's

changing already! Oh, Your Majesty, I'm disappointed in your choice of replacement—so little constancy. A few scratches and she loses the strength to keep the spell going!"

Rose felt the queen let go and realized why as she tried to hit the bird again. She had her own hands now, brownish and short-nailed, not the princess's pretty long fingers. She felt ashamed for a moment but decided that being carried away by a magic bird was a reasonable excuse.

Freddie and Bella suddenly appeared beside her, and she realized that they had crawled along under the tablecloth to get through the milling crowd.

"Help me!" she wailed to Freddie, and he hit the bird with a menu card, which did nothing at all.

"Use a spell," she whispered. The pain and the blood seeping from the deep wounds in her arm were making her feel faint, light-headed. Light—no, it would be easier for the bird to carry her up. She mustn't be light... Freddie nodded apologetically and reached out a shaking hand toward the bird, muttering under his breath and then slinging all his power against the glittering little creature in a ball of silvery light. Then he collapsed shuddering onto his knees, staring hopefully after his magic.

It didn't even reach the bird. The ice-eyed man clicked his fingers, and Freddie's silver magic froze and shattered into splinters, sending all Rose's would-be rescuers reeling back again.

"Rose, fight back!" Bella called urgently as she fought her way to Rose, brushing away the icy shards. Rose felt the little girl holding her other hand, sending all her childish power, and the fainting passed away at last. She opened her eyes wide and saw Gus, bigger than ever, erupting out of the roses with a massive leap.

The Talish envoy gasped in fury. Gus seized the bird, his own claws growing to the size of a tiger's and puncturing its metal skin.

It screamed, and Rose screamed with it as Gus dragged the jeweled claws out of her arm.

Together they fell onto the table, the huge white cat lunging to bite around the bird's pulsing neck and shake it violently. Rose sank back into her chair, cradling her arm, her breath shallow and fast. Freddie staggered over and put his arm around her shoulders, holding her as they watched Gus shake the bird until it hung limply in his teeth. Then he dragged it across the table to Rose.

Lord Venn watched, his face contorted with anger, and now everyone in the room was whispering and pointing at Rose, so that Freddie and Bella drew in closer to her, guarding her against the whispers. *Impostor…Traitor…A plot…*

Queen Adelaide was sobbing and hitting the king's arms, demanding in a thin, frightened voice that he tell her where Jane was.

"I'm sorry, Rose," Gus told her, as he laid the

mangled metal thing in her lap. "I was trying to call Aloysius. I couldn't find him—who knows where he's gone. I waited too long." He nosed her bleeding arm sorrowfully, and Rose felt the wounds close up a little.

With her good hand, she touched the bedraggled golden feathers and felt the faint heartbeat still inside the thing. "It's alive," she muttered, looking up at Gus, his whiskers drooping down over the creature. "Except, it's not. The spell is gone. Gus, there's a real bird in here!"

Suddenly angry, she tore into the golden skin, using Freddie and Bella to help her, and among the scraps of metal foil and the bloodied jewels, there was a sparrow—a little town sparrow, its black claws curled up, and its liquid eyes half closed. It shivered as its protective skin came off, and its eyes opened. Still surrounded by remnants of magic, it gazed at Rose. *Take me out of here! Don't let me die in here,* it pleaded, and she reached in to cradle it, so feather light she could hardly feel it in her hand.

*Thank you…*And the bird shivered and died, suddenly a ball of dusty feathers and no more.

Rose stood up, shaking off Freddie and Bella, forgetting the pain in her arm, clutching the dead bird against her chest. "You did this!" she hissed at the Talish envoy. "You made it! You shut a real bird in a metal prison to make a jewel to kill a princess."

"Except you are not a princess," Lord Venn pointed out coldly. "You are—some little witch that Aloysius

Fountain has bribed into his schemes. And now your whole court knows that dear Princess Jane is lost."

A gasp ran round the room, and he turned triumphantly to look out at the guests. "Oh, yes, ladies and gentlemen. They have no idea where she is." He smirked.

"Nonsense. Arrest this man!" the king stepped forward, one arm still around his wife, looking steadily around at his court as he lied to them. "Please, do not listen to these ravings. I admit, that as you can see, Princess Jane is not here. She is quite safe, hidden away from a kidnapping plot—a cruel attempt to bring our beloved country to its knees with grief. This brave child stood in Jane's place to protect her." He clapped his hands loudly, one man clapping in a sea of whispers. Freddie clapped too, very fast and nervously, and slowly, gradually, others joined in. But it was polite applause, forced by the king, and there was no real sense of celebration. No one knew what to believe.

"He's lying." Lord Venn laughed, staring at the confused courtiers. "The girl was under a glamour, a nasty, deceitful trick."

As the court muttered amongst themselves, Rose climbed onto the table, a ragged figure in the ruins of a pink silk dress, covered in bloodstains and clutching a dead bird. She towered over Lord Venn, and Bella scrambled up behind her. Gus leaped gracefully over to stand by her side, and Freddie cast an apologetic glance at the king and followed.

Obviously, the king was still trying to hide Jane's disappearance, so Rose didn't scream her accusations out loud, as she so wanted to. She shouted into the envoy's mind instead, making him flinch away from the unavoidable words.

You stole her! You stole her once and you lost her, and you stole her again. Give her back! Give me her back!

"Stupid girl!" he spat, stumbling away with his hands over his ears. "We never took her."

The ice-eyed man stepped forward as though to hush him, as though Rose's fury was making Lord Venn forget his part, as though he was telling truths no one was meant to hear.

"Be silent, fool!" he snarled.

Where is she? Rose screamed silently, leeching all Freddie and Bella's magic from them and coiling it with her own to hurl at Lord Venn. He was almost at breaking point; she was sure she only needed to press a little harder.

The ice-eyed man shot her a malevolent glare and seized Lord Venn's arm, but the fat little man struggled violently.

"It's him in charge, not Venn, look," Freddie muttered.

"He made the snow globes," Rose gasped out. She could hardly speak it was taking so much energy to pour the magic into Lord Venn's skin. "He's the one with the winter magic. He's so cold, Freddie, he's burning me!"

"The snow globe…" Rose felt Freddie's power waver.

"Rose, I gave it to Mr. Fountain!"

"Aloysius!" Gus moaned in anguish. "I couldn't find him! Aloysius, what have they done to you?" He leaped onto Rose's shoulder and stood staring down at Lord Venn and the ice magician, and Rose sobbed as she felt the power in her suddenly grow and grow, until she ached with it.

"She's still here!" the envoy gasped, his eyes rolling in agony, torn between Rose and the ice-eyed man. But it was the last thing he said. His master wrapped his arms around him and closed his ice-blue eyes. Lord Venn went white but not with pain—he was covered in a sudden coating of enchanted frost, glazing him all over. He cast a last beseeching glance at Rose before the ice covered his face, there was a strange splintering, crackling noise, and the pair of them disappeared, leaving a few silvery snowflakes floating gently down.

Most of the guests screamed, and Rose and the others stared down at the empty space where the two men had been. Rose staggered slightly, the anger and strength she'd drawn from the sparrow's unwilling sacrifice flooding away. Freddie caught her as she slumped onto the tablecloth, a small, bloodied heap amongst the silverware.

Fifteen

ROSE WOKE UP IN Princess Jane's bed, wearing her nightgown, and with Princess Charlotte curled up next to her. She blinked wearily. Had the glamour somehow come back? Did everyone think she was Jane again?

"Look, she moved!" Bella's face suddenly appeared in front of her, looking worried. "Rose, can you see me? Are you there?"

"Of course I am…" Rose murmured. It seemed such a silly question. Where else would she be?

"We thought you were dead," Freddie muttered. Rose peered down and saw him sitting hunched at the end of the bed. "You fell down, after Lord Venn and the other one disappeared, and we couldn't wake you. You didn't even move. I got Raph to carry you up here, and Bella undressed you. Gus told me a spell to help your arm heal, and we all put the last of our strength into it, but you just lay there, and we couldn't even see you breathing."

"I shouldn't be here…" Rose batted feebly at Jane's bedclothes.

"We didn't know where else to take you," Freddie told her miserably. "The whole palace is running around whispering about where Jane is and who you really are and whether it's all a huge conspiracy—"

"It is," Rose pointed out. "The king's conspiracy." She gave a grim little smile. "But I wouldn't put it past him to throw the blame on us if he can't make it all work out. I suppose he's doing it for the good of the country, but he lied to everyone at the banquet last night. Actually, he started lying as soon as he let us use the glamour if you think about it."

Freddie looked uncomfortable but nodded. "He was doing it for good reasons," he protested.

"I don't know how much longer it will be safe to stay here," Gus said quietly. He was sitting on the windowsill, staring down into the gardens. "There are a great many people gathering at the gates. I don't think the king's assurance last night that Jane is safe was quite convincing enough. Not after the little show that Venn and his master put on."

Freddie scrambled off the bed and went to look too.

"It's a riot," he said fearfully. "What do they want?"

"Jane." Gus looked round at Rose. "The real one." He closed his eyes and listened. "They're shouting that she has been stolen, and the king has lied. They want to see her."

"How would they know she was the real one, anyway?" Rose asked. "Haven't we just stopped people believing anyone is who they say they are?"

Freddie looked doubtful. "Well, if you stood next to her…What does it matter, though? We don't know where she is!"

"Lord Venn said she'd never left the palace," Rose reminded him.

"Venn! He was deranged!" Freddie spat.

Rose shook her head. "I'm sure he was telling the truth. He didn't want to say it, I could tell. That's why the ice-eyed man took him away—he was telling us too much." She blinked thoughtfully. "He said that we were all plotting with Mr. Fountain," she remembered, the pictures of last night trickling slowly back into her mind. "He knew him, or knew of him, anyway. Where is your father, Bella?"

"Searching for the princess, of course," Bella snapped too quickly.

"We don't know," Freddie told her in a low voice. "No one knows…I gave him the snow globe, Rose, like he asked. We've all called him, but he hasn't come. I wish he'd hurry."

Gus's tail twitched frantically over by the window, and Rose saw that none of them could bear to say it—that maybe Mr. Fountain wouldn't come. That he couldn't.

Rose sat up painfully. "I can't just lie here," she told

them. "I have to get up. We have to find out what's going on. It isn't safe just hiding up here."

A sudden scratching at the door made them all jump, and Freddie's foolish cousin, Raph, peered around the edge, his beautiful white-and-gold uniform torn and grubby. "Oh good, you're here. Freddie, I think you should take your friends back to your father's house. You'll be safer there." He looked back at the door behind him anxiously. "No one knows what's going on. It was all some strange Talish plot, but the rest of the envoy's staff swear that the emperor didn't send him to do this, and Venn and that strange deputy of his had them all bewitched. The king has had Venn's rooms searched, and they've found plans to invade. The ice on the river, it was just the beginning. He wanted to freeze the sea, can you imagine? All the way to the capital, Sevina, so the emperor's army could just march here across the ice to take the city. It's all melting out there already, you know.

"One of the Talish admitted that Venn stole the princess to distract everyone from what was really happening and throw suspicion on the magicians who were the only ones who might be able to stop him."

"It would be hard to fight a war with no more alchemical gold," Freddie muttered.

"Better get them away, Freddie," Raph said, staring out of the window. "Soon. Venn's gone, but his plan's still working. Everyone's terrified."

"No! You mustn't go!" Charlotte had woken up without them realizing, and now she threw her arms around Rose and held her tight. She cried furiously, hitting at Rose with her hands and then clinging to her again. "Don't go, don't go!"

"I won't, I promise. Charlotte, stop hitting. It hurts." Rose put her good arm around the child's heaving shoulders.

"Rose, we have to!" Freddie hissed.

"I can't leave her! No one else seems to have thought about her—where are all the ladies-in-waiting?" Rose demanded.

"Spreading rumors," Raph put in. "Telling everyone they always suspected you. Making sure no one can blame them for any of this mess."

Gus chuckled at this, and Rose looked at Raph sharply. He didn't seem nearly as stupid as she'd been told.

"They probably thought she was still asleep," Freddie said thoughtfully, looking at Charlotte. "She came looking for you a couple hours ago, and she wouldn't go back to her own room. It's not even six now."

"I don't care!" Charlotte stuck out her lower lip. "I want to get up, and I want Rose to play with me. She plays better than Jane does anyway."

Rose slid carefully out of the bed, and let Bella help her put on Jane's dressing gown. "You two should go," she told Freddie and Bella. "I don't think anyone will let me slip out of here, will they? After last night?"

Freddie sighed. "No, probably not. Well, I'm staying then. Come on. What are we playing?"

"The dollhouse!" Charlotte squealed, and she ran into the drawing room, leaving the others to trail after her. Raph muttered something about having to stay and guard the princess, and followed them.

Freddie and Gus sat on the window seat, still watching the growing crowd and muttering anxiously together while Bella and Rose and Charlotte played—or Charlotte did, and Bella and Rose tried not to wonder what the running footsteps in the corridors outside meant.

Charlotte was organizing a grand party, putting all the dolls into the ballroom and making them dance.

"Oh, Rose, look! She can't go to the party. She's got her nightgown on. How funny, she'll have to be sick in bed." And Charlotte plucked the fair-haired doll out of the dancing and stood up to reach to the bedroom floors.

Rose blinked. There hadn't been a doll in a nightgown before. She was sure there hadn't. "Charlotte, can I see her?" she asked urgently, but the little girl clutched the doll close and pouted. Rose forced herself to smile. "I want to see if she's got spots!" she whispered, and Charlotte giggled and sat down next to her, holding out the doll.

"Oh, dear, dear me," Rose murmured, hardly listening to herself as she stared at the china doll. "Mumps. And measles, and the whooping cough…"

"What else?" Charlotte demanded, snuggling up against her.

"Ummm, the smallpox and a broken leg...Bella, look..."

Bella peered at the doll and sighed. "Influenza. You shouldn't humor her like this, Rose. She'll go on wanting this game for ages, and I can't think of any others."

"No, look." Rose stroked the light-colored hair. "She wasn't there before, Bella. I haven't played with the house for the last two days—except—yes. Of course. This is the doll that was lying on the floor. The one Gus told me off for tidying up just after we made the glamour."

"What?" Gus leaped lightly off the window seat and came to sniff the doll.

"All her legs broken!" Charlotte begged, but they weren't listening. "Ro-ose!"

Rose held the doll out to her. "Charlotte, have you seen this one before? Don't you think she looks like Jane?"

Charlotte sniffed crossly and pulled up the sleeve of the doll's nightgown. "Yes, because look, she's got that funny mark. Now tell me what else she's sick with!"

It was true. The china arm was marred with an odd brown blotch.

"Jane had a birthmark?" Freddie asked. "It's a good thing no one checked that on you, Rose."

Rose nodded. "All those times Lady Alice saw me in

my petticoats," she murmured. "No one ever looked when they were dressing me. Why a doll, do you think? Just because he could?"

"To tease?" Freddie suggested. "So everyone's searching for her, and she's here all the time? Venn seemed mad enough for that."

"You interrupted them," Gus said, sniffing the china hair carefully. "This wasn't what they intended."

"How do we get her back?" Bella asked, staring doubtfully at the doll.

Everyone looked at the Jane doll lying limply in Rose's lap. She did not look as though she had ever really been human. Now Rose examined her closely, it was obvious that she was much more finely painted than the other dolls. Even dolls that belonged to a princess did not have that sort of coloring, hair painted with so many tiny brush strokes. Jane made a pretty doll though—that rather lifeless face, so used to looking polite and well behaved that it hardly ever moved. And now it couldn't.

"What would happen if we broke it?" Freddie asked, frowning down at her.

"No!" Charlotte squeaked, snatching Jane up and hugging her. Rose wasn't sure if she realized that this was actually her sister or if she was merely horrified at the idea of breaking a doll.

"But it might set her free!" Freddie explained. "Breaking the spell, you see."

"Or it might mean no one could ever bring her back," Bella snapped. "We don't know!"

"Do you think she's actually in there? Inside, I mean? A tiny version of her?" Rose asked. "I don't really understand how this works. Is it like you being that little gold charm cat, Gus?"

Gus sniffed the doll, waving his tail around Charlotte's nose and making her giggle reluctantly. "It depends on the spell that was used to do it. I changed myself, making me into something different. She was forced." He licked the china cheek with his pink tongue, very delicately. "This only looks like china. It tastes like child. She's there." He shivered. "She's held with ice magic, I think. Frozen into shape. No, we mustn't break her. I think we ought to melt her."

Rose looked at the fire and shuddered. "If it was the ice-eyed man who did it—and the winter was his too—ice would make sense. Freddie, do you think my fiery monster would melt magic ice?"

Freddie nodded slowly. "I wish Mr. Fountain were here," he murmured. "I don't think we have time to wait for him," he added, glancing over at the window as a particularly loud shout echoed from the palace grounds. "You could try."

Charlotte would not let go of the doll, so Rose took the little girl on her lap and held Jane with her. "Everyone think about her—like you did for the glamour," she said, staring into the heart of the drawing-room fire. She could feel the warmth on her face, and she closed her eyes, remembering the yellow-white glow where the fire was hottest, and crumbling red shards of coal, turning them into something else. Not a frightening monster like the one she'd planned to use against the kidnappers but a soft creature—a fire cat, as Jane's father had said she liked cats. Its silky flame-fur wrapped lovingly around the doll, yellow eyes beseeching her to come out and play. It twitched its tail across her face as Gus had done to Charlotte only moments before and curled warmly into her lap.

Rose opened her eyes slowly, not sure whether it had worked. No one had said anything, which probably meant it hadn't. But Charlotte wasn't on her lap anymore, she realized, shaking her head wearily. She was sitting in the midst of the circle of staring children, leaning against Princess Jane, and together they were stroking a cat, a strange ash-gray cat, who seemed to be shrinking and fading as Rose's thoughts cleared.

"Oh, bring him back," Jane said sadly, as he disappeared at last. "He found me and brought me home. Where is he going, Rose?"

"He wasn't real, Your Highness," Gus purred, staring into her eyes. "Rose made him from firelight to rescue you. You could stroke me instead," he added hopefully, and the princess gave a little gasp of a laugh at this strange talking cat and patted him cautiously.

* * *

"You had better wear one of my dresses," the princess told Rose critically. "You can't appear to the populace in that."

Rose looked at her green wool frock. It seemed perfectly good to her, but she supposed her standards were different. "Your dresses wouldn't fit me, Your Highness," she pointed out.

Jane frowned. "So you can rescue me from an evil magician, but you can't stretch a dress?" she asked rather disgustedly.

"She hasn't time to change anyway, Your Highness," Gus pointed out. "I'll glamour her." And before Rose could protest, Gus was in her arms, and she was dressed in a gray silk dress, with a little jacket trimmed in white fur. "Now you match me very nicely," the white cat told her smugly. "Don't put me down, or it will all disappear."

"Like Cinderella!" Princess Jane murmured, and Rose sighed.

As soon as the princess had returned, Raphael had raced off to find the king, and the princesses' rooms had been filled with people. King Albert had swept his daughter up in his arms, holding her as though he didn't dare let her go, but at last one of his advisers had gently pointed out that the crowd was still screaming outside. The only way to quiet them was to show them the princess. Both princesses—Jane and Rose.

Which was why they were waiting in this drafty gallery, half listening to a long speech that was going on outside, and Rose was now wearing a dress fit for a princess.

"Listen." Gus nudged Rose's chin. "You'll be on in a minute."

"My dearest daughter, Princess Jane, and the dear child who bravely agreed to protect her from a Talish assassin."

Lady Alice hustled them out to stand next to the king and queen as Gus muttered, "No mention for me?" and Rose stared blankly at a sea of people spread out below her, silently staring.

"They're not sure what to believe," Freddie murmured from his place behind Rose.

"They will believe in *me*," Jane said with a regal certainty, and she took Rose's hand and led her forward to the very front of the balcony. Then she placed one hand on each side of her face and very seriously kissed her cheek, before turning her to face the crowd, her arm around her.

In a clear, loud voice, Jane called down to the muttering crowd. "This girl is a magician who risked her life to save mine. There was a magical plot to abduct me, and she and her companions foiled it and saved our country from a madman. Believe me, dear friends, when I ask you to trust in her and all her kind."

It was very much what the king had been saying, but

on Jane's lips it carried far more power for the crowd, and there was only a moment of measuring silence before they roared their approval. It was that same magic that the king had borne for Freddie and herself, Rose saw, a strange kind of charm, half the child, and half the history behind her, adding up to a potent and binding spell.

Jane bowed and waved graciously several times, nudging Rose to do the same, before she withdrew back into the gallery, and Rose collapsed limply onto a velvet bench.

"You did well," someone said behind her, and Rose gasped. "Where have you been? I'm sorry, sir, I mean…" Mr. Fountain was standing at the door to the balcony, looking pale and weary, with Isabella in his arms.

"The snow globe," he explained. "I had it in my hand, Rose, when Venn revealed himself at the banquet. I was so close to finding the secret of the winter spell, or so I thought, that I stayed in my rooms, leaving you and Gus and Freddie and Bella to work the glamour. I'm still not sure where it took me. It was so cold my mind seemed to stop." He shivered.

Rose nodded emphatically. "Yes, it was like that for me too when I tried to stop Princess Jane being kidnapped. And the cold burned."

"We searched for you, sir," Freddie told him. "You weren't in your room, and Gus couldn't feel you anywhere."

Mr. Fountain smiled at them. "I don't know how many of those snow globes there were, but they were the seeds of the spell. Pretty little things in houses all through the city, spreading the cold. He was very clever."

"But Rose beat him," Freddie objected. "I don't mean it like that," he added quickly. "Venn just didn't seem all that clever when we fought him at the banquet."

Mr. Fountain shook his head. "It wasn't him." Gus laid his ears back and shivered.

"Venn was only the front man," Mr. Fountain explained. "I've met him, and that winter magic wasn't his. You can tell. The feel was wrong, the taste of it. It was the other one…"

"The ice-eyed man," Rose whispered. "I thought so. He made them, didn't he? It was him who gave me that one, at the Frost Fair. Who is he?"

"I don't know." Mr. Fountain sighed. "I thought I knew all the most powerful magicians in Europe, but I've never met him. I think we may have to find out. They ran, Rose, but they aren't beaten—although Venn may never be the same again. They won't give up, and that spell wasn't just about stealing a princess. It was power they wanted. Venn must have worked his way into the emperor's trust, and that would have taken time. I'm sure if their plan had worked, the emperor would have been delighted to take advantage of it. But I shouldn't think the emperor would have lasted very long after that—or only in name, anyway. Venn would have been his closest counselor, and the ice magician would have been controlling Venn. The strength of that spell…it was incredible. The snow globe held me for half a day, and for much of that time I couldn't even think, even after they'd fled."

"What happened to it?" Rose asked.

Mr. Fountain reached into his waistcoat pocket and drew out a glittering glass ornament, specks of silvery snow whirling inside it. "It isn't the same, I'm afraid," he told her.

He was right. It was only a trinket now, a toy. The skaters didn't move, and the snow was only glitter. But if Rose half closed her eyes, she could remember how it was before, and it was very, very beautiful.

Turn the page for the next
book in the spellbinding
Rose series:

Rose

and the Magician's Mask

$\mathcal{E}$VEN AFTER LIVING THERE, the palace was still a breathtaking sight. It reminded Rose of a cake—the sort of fine white wedding cake that the smart confectioners had in their windows, all crusted with swags of sugar icing.

An anxious-looking young man in an ornate uniform was pacing up and down the mews, clearly waiting for them, and Freddie moaned at the sight of him. "Oh, no. Raph's done something awful again. Look at him, he's almost green."

Raphael Cressy was Freddie's cousin, an equerry to the king. No one was quite sure how he'd ever been given the post, but Freddie believed it was because his regiment were prepared to lie through their teeth to make sure he never went near the front line.

Raph was startlingly beautiful, and so he was useful at the palace in a decorative sort of way—all Princess Jane's older sisters were in love with him. Quite unfairly, his good looks often got him out of trouble, but he was terribly dim most of the time.

Raph dashed to open the carriage door, almost colliding with the coachman, who retired to his box, muttering.

"Please hurry, sir," he begged. "His Majesty is beside himself with worry."

"What did you do, you idiot?" Freddie hissed, jumping down, and handing Rose out.

"It wasn't me!" Raph protested. "Really, I never went anywhere near the thing. His Majesty's waiting in the throne room, do come on." He seized Rose's sleeve, and actually pulled her inside past the guards, hustling the party up an enormous staircase, the banisters held up by plump and winsome cherubs that had Mr. Fountain wincing. He strongly disapproved of many of the king's renovations. "The throne room," he was muttering. "It would be. All that scarlet carpet gives me such a headache, and the statues are absurd." Gus ran ahead of Raph, his tail waving high. He adored dramatic situations, and Rose suspected he was also hoping to finally have a chance to terrorize Queen Adelaide's lap dog. Gus had been in disguise during most of their previous visit, and had been forced to control his natural instincts.

The king was pacing up and down the scarlet carpet that had so worried Mr. Fountain. Rose agreed—the carpet was blood-colored, and the walls were a shade darker. It was like being inside a bag of liver, which had been liberally dotted with gilded marble statues. It was also unfortunate that the king was wearing a crimson Guards' uniform which clashed, subtly and dreadfully. He looked haggard, his face grayish pale, and his eyes haunted.

"At last!"

"I'm so sorry, Sire, we came as soon as the message arrived. It's really gone?"

"Look!" The king wheeled round and pointed dramatically at a display of weapons on the wall. Even Rose could see that there was a rather unfortunate gap in the middle.

"Is this mask supposed to be there?" she hissed to Freddie.

Freddie shrugged. He looked put out, as he prided himself on knowing more about the palace than Rose did.

"Why are those *children* here?" Queen Adelaide was sweeping down the room toward them, the train of her velvet dress trailing across the red carpet. Behind her trotted a grumpy-looking pageboy, carrying her fat little Pekingese dog, its eyes bulging at the sight of Gus.

"We need their help, my dear," the king reminded her curtly.

Rose bent her knees slightly, hoping to hide the inches of leg that showed under her outgrown dress. But she could tell that the queen could see what she was doing. Queen Adelaide looked down her rather long nose at the two children. "Do they have to look quite so *disheveled*?" she asked in a stagey sort of whisper.

Mr. Fountain bowed. He didn't like the queen, it was quite obvious—though he was far too much the courtier to admit any such thing. "We obeyed His Majesty's summons in rather a hurry, ma'am."

The queen's "Hmmm" was masterly, and Rose and Freddie both attempted to hide behind Mr. Fountain. This meant that Gus came out from around his master's legs, and leered at the Pekingese. The Peke stood up in the pageboy's arms and barked itself silly, while Gus merely stared demurely at it, standing decoratively next to Rose and opening his eyes very wide. He knew that made him look innocent, but Rose could tell from the twitching of his tail-tip that he was enjoying himself enormously.

The queen seized the Peke from the pageboy and cooed lovingly at it, but the little creature fought and scrabbled, yapping hysterically.

I think he is being terribly rude in Chinese, Gus told Rose admiringly. *I wish I understood.*

At last the queen handed the dog back to the pageboy, still wriggling frantically. "I shall have to take Flower out of here," the queen pronounced, frowning. "He cannot stand to associate with such an underbred animal. I will speak to you later, my dear." She processed out, with the pageboy following her, stuffing Flower inside his gilt-encrusted jacket, and glowering at Rose and Freddie, who were stifling giggles.

"Did she mean me?" Gus was staring after the queen, an expression of amazement and dawning horror in his eyes. "Underbred? Me?"

The king had heard Gus talk before, but he still jumped slightly as the voice echoed from around his feet. "I'm so sorry," he said awkwardly—clearly finding it hard to address a cat, even one as grand as Gus. "My wife is not fond of cats. I am quite sure you have a magnificent pedigree." Tentatively he reached out to pat Gus's head, but something about the way Rose, Freddie and Mr. Fountain all sucked in a breath made him withdraw his hand again.

"I am descended from an Egyptian god," Gus snapped, his tail lashing to and fro.

"Sire, what is the magician's mask?" Rose asked, bobbing a curtsey in the direction of the king. Showing her ignorance didn't weigh against distracting Gus from clawing the reigning monarch.

"An heirloom…" King Albert gazed at the space on the wall, a dazed expression settling in his eyes. "A mask, made of gold, and inlaid with enamelling and gems. Unbelievably precious, even as a jewel…"

"Except it isn't just a jewel," Mr. Fountain sighed. "It's a magical tool, a Venetian mask. It's well known that the Venetians have strange powers, and they hold magical festivities, with *interesting* dancing. Rituals, you know. Foreign cults are mixed up with it all," he added vaguely. "Priests travel from the far Indies to be there, so I've been told."

"Probably the ones that worshipped me," Gus snarled.

"Mmm. I've often wondered about going to Venice. Masks, most fascinating things, and the Venetian masks are known to have incredible powers for the wearer... And as if that isn't enough, this particular mask belonged to Dr. Dee, Queen Elizabeth's court magician. He was said to have learned many of his strange powers in Venice. Who knows what spells he imbued it with, besides its own secrets? It's an invaluable magical artifact."

The king, flushed spots burning along his high cheekbones, drew something out of his waistcoat.

Everyone stared at him politely. Eventually, Freddie ventured, "That's a teaspoon, Sire." He exchanged a worried sideways glance with Rose. Missing princesses were one thing—an insane king was quite another.

"I know that," the king murmured patiently. "Earlier this afternoon, one of the butlers discovered that the display above you now contained a teaspoon—this teaspoon—instead of Dr. Dee's mask."

Mr. Fountain took the spoon, weighing it in his hand. "It's been glamoured," he said, tapping it against his teeth, and then biting it gently. "The theft didn't happen yesterday." He eyed the king thoughtfully, obviously wondering if he needed to explain.

"Well, of course it didn't!" the king exclaimed irritably. "It was that cad Venn and his accomplice. Obviously! Who else has been dallying about the palace with unlimited magical powers? And look at the handle. Unbelievable conceit. The gall of it. They left their calling card."

Rose peered over at the teaspoon, and Gus, curiosity winning over dignified fury, leaped into her arms to see too. Delicately etched into the silver handle of the spoon was an intricate snowflake.

Rose frowned. It seemed a lot of effort for Gossamer and Lord Venn to go to. All this for something that was just for dressing up?

"What will they do with the mask?" she asked, nibbling at one of her nails. "Does it—does it *do* anything?"

"If they can unravel the secrets of its spells, they can do whatever they like," Mr. Fountain muttered, slumping onto one of the spindly gilt chairs, and wiping a silk handkerchief across his forehead. "It's terribly powerful. But then, no one since Dee has really known how to use it. No one has dared to wear it, not knowing what would happen." There was a strange longing in his voice, and his eyes were hidden by the handkerchief. "I need to go home and look it all up—I have a history of Venice somewhere. There are rituals. Certain days when everyone wears masks. But this mask—the right person could wear it to wreak havoc, and remain a secret. Or, even worse, he could use it to create. To build."

"To build an army," the king said in a low voice. He didn't even bother with a chair, just sank down on the pedestal of one of the ugly gilded statues. "An army of magicians, following the power of the masked man."

"We wouldn't…" But Mr. Fountain sounded doubtful, and he shivered, and smiled faintly, one hand stroking across his cheek, as though he was smoothing on a mask.

Mr. Fountain stayed silent for almost the whole of the coach journey home. Freddie and Rose exchanged curious glances, but somehow the silence infected them too, and they didn't dare to break it. Even Gus perched on Mr. Fountain's shoulder and glared out of the window at the darkening streets.

About the Author

Holly Webb was born and grew up in southeast London but spent a lot of time on the Suffolk coast. As a child, she had two dogs, a cat, and at one point, nine gerbils (an accident). At about ten, Holly fell in love with stories from Ancient Greek myths, which led to studying Latin and Greek, and eventually to reading Classics at university. She worked for five years as a children's fiction editor before deciding that writing was more fun and easier to do from a sofa. Now living in Reading with her husband, three sons, and two cats, Holly runs a Girl Scout unit. The Rose books stem from a childhood love of historical novels and the wish that animals really could talk.